I0580918

When we think of artistic interpretations of Dante Alighieri's Inferno we are bound to recall William Blake's lovely watercolors or Gustav Doré's elegant engravings, but never has Dante's vision been rendered with such an unflinching eye for the epic poem's horrific and grotesque imagery as in the numerous illustrations Jim Agpalza has crafted for this edition. Here, presented in a bold style both modern and classical, are the nightmarish spectacles one might truly expect to encounter in the torturous nine circles of Hell. Agpalza's work is as disturbing as it is imaginative, and along with the crisp interior design makes this edition of the Inferno something to treasure.

—JEFFREY THOMAS
author of Punktown

There is no greater undertaking for an artist than to guide us through Hell, and no better guide this side of Virgil than Jim Agpalza. Like his predecessor Gustave Dore, Jim has leveraged his peculiar genius for caricature into a transcendent vision of torment and suffering when we thought we'd seen it all. For his efforts, Dore was knighted and inducted into the Legion d'honneur at the end of his life. We should be ashamed to honor Jim Agpalza with anything less.

—CODY GOODFELLOW
author of Unamerica and Strategies Against Nature

PRAISE FOR THE INFERNO

The man himself acted like God as a critic, consigning the Florentine artist Cimabue to Purgatory, supposedly for his arrogance, so Doré was fortunate not to be immortalized by Dante. Chiaroscuro was three hundred years in the future (and Dante didn't know how to time-travel), so I think Dante would have loved Mike Dubisch's gorgeous poster (it makes me think of Fruosino warping not only R. Crumb but Mad's Jack Davis with the Tibetan Cave murals of Chakrasamvara. Quite Boschian in recreational activities, this sings Dante in the palette of his time as a bonus.

In contrast, Jim Agpalza's cover features one of the beasts so much more interesting than the face of God in Heaven, and lo! the beast is in that to-die-for blue Florentines like Dante so loved. The illustrations take as a starting block, Doré, and go beyond, to where only this superb artist can steal you off to.

—ANNA TAMBOUR
author of Death Goes to the Dogs

For people of a certain bent, that is, people like me, this stunning new edition of The Inferno, enriched by Jim Agpalza's gleefully lurid illustrations, is now the definitive edition of Dante's dark masterpiece.

—MATTHEW M. BARTLETT
author of Gateways to Abomination

THE
INFERNO

with an introduction by Anna Tambour

Written by
Dante Alighieri
Translated by
James Romanes Sibbald
with insights from
Rev. Henry Francis Cary, M. A.
and illustrations by
Jim Agpalza

MMXXII
MOSS BEACH
PUBLISHED BY ODDNESS
MDCCCLXXXIV

THE
INFERNO

Published by ODDNESS

www.forbiddenfutures.com

Art Copyright © 2022 by Jim Agpalza

Ordering Information:
For details, contact unclekrust@forbiddenfutures.com

Softback (Clean) ISBN: 978-1-7322124-2-8
Hardback (Dirty) ISBN: 978-1-7322124-3-5

Printed in the United States of America on SFI Certified paper.

First Edition

NOTE FROM
THE PUBLISHER

The Forbidden Futures presentation of Dante Alighieri's The Inferno was carefully transcribed word by word from the James Romanes Sibbald 1884 edition and complimented with the canto arguments of Rev. Henry Francis Cary, M.A., another noted translator of The Divine Comedy.

Within these pages, one will discover Jim Agpalza's masterfully striking interpretation of The Inferno blended with 19th century and modern typography styles and a helpful guide disguised as a table of contents. Kindly look to other versions to find the footnotes and prefaces sought.

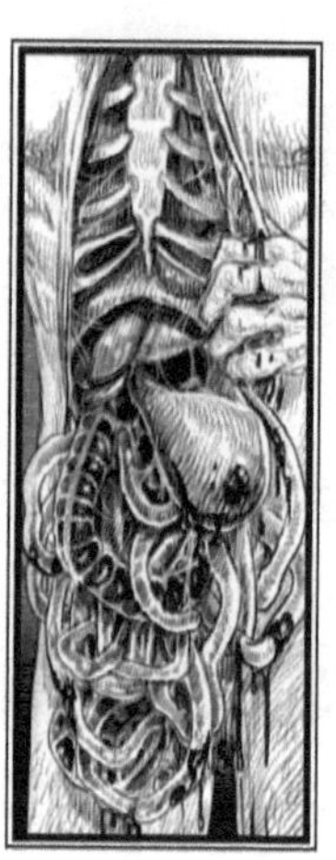

CONTENTS

The Forest
The writer, having lost his way in a gloomy forest, and being hindered by certain wild beasts from ascending a mountain, is met by Virgil, who promises to show him the punishment of Hell, and afterward of purgatory; and that he shall then be conducted by Beatrice into Paradise. He follows the Roman poet.

Virgil's Mission
After the invocation, which poets are used to prefix to their works, he shows that, on a consideration of his own strength, he doubted whether it sufficed for the journey proposed to him, but that being comforted by Virgil, he at last took courage, and followed him as his guide and master.

CANTO III

<u>The Vestibule</u>

After the invocation, which poets are used to prefix to their works, he shows that, on a consideration of his own strength, he doubted whether it sufficed for the journey proposed to him, but that being comforted by Virgil, he at last took courage, and followed him as his guide and master.

CANTO IV

<u>The First Circle</u>

The Poet, being roused by a clap of thunder, and following his guide onward, descends into Limbo, which is the first circle of Hell, where he finds the souls of those, who, although they have lived virtuously and have not to suffer for great sins, nevertheless, through lack of baptism, merit not the bliss of Paradise. Hence he is led on by Virgil to descend into the second circle.

CANTO VII

p. 36 - 42

The Fourth Circle

In the present Canto, Dante describes his descent into the fourth circle, at the beginning of which he sees Plutus stationed. Here one like doom awaits the prodigal and the avaricious; which is, to meet in direful conflict, rolling great weights against each other with mutual upbraidings. From hence Virgil takes occasion to show how vain the goods that are committed into the charge of Fortune; and this moves out author to inquire what being that Fortune is, of whom he speaks: which question being resolved they go down into the fifth circle, where they find the wrathful and gloomy tormented in the Stygian Lake. Having make a compass round a great part of this lake, they come at last to the base of a lofty tower.

Scenes	*Lines*
Plutus	*1 - 13*
Misers and Spendthrifts	*14 - 54*
Fortune	*55 - 90*
Styx	*91 - 115*
The Wrathful	*116 - 130*

Illustrations	
Plutus	*35*
Misers and Spendthrifts	*38*
The Wrathful	*41*

CANTO VIII

p. 43 - 48

The Fifth Circle

A signal having been made from the tower, Phlegyas, the ferryman of the lake, speedily crosses it, and conveys Virgil and Dante to the other side. On their passage, they meet with Filippo Argenti whose fury and torment are described. They then arrive at the city of Dis, the entrance whereto is denied, and the portals closed against them by many Demons.

Scenes	*Lines*
The Watch Tower	*1 - 13*
Phlegyas	*14 - 36*
Philip Argenti	*37 - 61*
The City of Dis	*62 - 72*
The Demons	*73 - 99*
The Rebuff	*100 - 130*

Illustrations	
Phlegyas	*44*

CANTO IX

<u>The Sixth Circle</u>
After some hindrances, and having seen the hellish furies and other monsters, the Poet, by the help of an angel, enters the city of Dis, wherein he discovers that the heretics are punished in tombs burnings with intense fire: and he, together with Virgil, passes onward between the sepulchers and the walls of the city.

CANTO X

<u>The Sixth Circle</u>
Dante, having obtained permission from his guide, holds discourse with Farinata degli Uberti and Cavalcante Cavalcanti, who lie in their fiery tombs that are yet open, and not to be closed up till after the last judgment. Farinata predicts the Poet's exile from Florence; and shows him that the condemned have knowledge of future things, but are ignorant of what is at present passing, unless it be revealed by some new-comer from earth.

CANTO XI   p. 61 - 64

<u>The Sixth Circle</u>
Dante arrives at the verge of a rocky precipice which encloses the seventh
circle, where he sees the sepulcher of Anastasius the Heretic; behind the lid
of which, pausing a little, to make himself capable by degrees of enduring the
fetid smell that steamed upward from the abyss, he is instructed by Virgil
concerning the manner in which the three following circles are disposed, and
what description of sinners is punished in each. He then inquires the reason
why the carnal, the gluttonous, the avaricious and prodigal, the wrathful and
gloomy, suffer not their punishments with the city of Dis. He next asks how
the crime of usury is an offence against God; and at length the two Poets go
toward the place from whence a passage leads down to the seventh circle.

<u>*Scenes*</u>   <u>*Lines*</u>
Pope Anastasius   *1 - 12*
The Kinds of Sin   *13 - 27*
Divisions of Inferno   *28 - 49*
The Kinds of Sin   *50 - 73*
Divisions of Inferno   *74 - 94*
Usury/The Advance   *95 - 115*

<u>*Illustrations*</u>
Pope Anastasius   *62*

CANTO XII   p. 65 - 71

<u>The Seventh Circle - The First Division</u>
Descending by a very rugged way into the seventh circle, where the vio-
lent are punished, Dante and his leader find it guarded by the Minotaur;
whose fury being pacified by Virgil, they step downward from crag to
crag; till, drawing near the bottom, they descry a river of blood, where-
in are tormented such as committed violence against their neighbor. At
these, where they strive to emerge from the blood, a troop of Centaurs,
running along the side of the river, aim their arrows; and three of their
band opposing our travelers at the foot of the steep, Virgil prevails so
far, that one consents to carry them both across the stream; and on their
passage Dante is informed by him of the course of the river, and of those
that are punished therein.

<u>*Scenes*</u>   <u>*Lines*</u>
The Rough Descent   *1 - 12*
The Minotaur   *12 - 36*
The Violent   *37 - 57*
The Centaurs   *58 - 84*
The Tyrants   *85 - 110*
Guy of Montfort   *111 - 120*
The Tyrants   *121 - 139*

<u>*Illustrations*</u>
The Minotaur   *66*
The Centaurs   *68*
The Tyrants   *70*

CONTENTS

<u>The Seventh Circle - The Second Division</u>
Still in the seventh circle, Dante enters its second compartment, which contains both those who have done violence on their own persons and those who have violently consumed their goods; the first changed into rough and knotted trees whereon the harpies build their nests, the latter chased and torn by black female mastiffs. Among the former, Piero delle Vigne is one who tells him the cause of his having committed suicide, and moreover in what manner the souls are transformed into those trunks. Of the latter crew, he recognizes Lano, a Siennese, and Giacomo, a Paduan: and lastly, a Florentine, who had hung himself form his own roof, speaks to him of the calamities of his countrymen.

<u>The Seventh Circle - The Third Division</u>
They arrive at the beginning of the third of those compartments into which this seventh circle is divided. It is a plain of dry and hot sand, where three kings of violence are punished; namely, against God, against Nature, and against Art; and those who may have thus sinned are tormented by flakes of fire, which are eternally showering down upon them. Among the violent against God is found Capaneus, whose blasphemies they hear. Next, turning to the left along the forest of self-slayers, and having journeyed a little onward, they meet with a streamlet of blood that issues from the forest and traverses the sandy plain. Here Virgil speaks to our Poet of a huge ancient statue that stands within Mount Ida in Crete, from a fissure in which statue there is a dripping of tears, from which the said streamlet, together with the three other infernal rivers, are formed.

CANTO XV

<u>The Seventh Circle</u>
Taking their way upon one of the mounds by which the streamlet, spoken of in the last Canto, was embanked, and having gone so far that they could no longer have discerned the forest if they had turned around to look for it, they meet a troop of spirits that come along the sand by the side of the pier. These are they who have done violence to Nature; and among Dante distinguishes Brunetto Latini, who had been formerly his master; with whom, turning a little backward, he holds a discourse which occupies the remainder of this Canto.

CANTO XVI

<u>The Seventh Circle</u>
Journeying along the pier, which crosses the sand, they are now so near the end of it as to hear the noise of the stream falling into the eighth circle, when they meet the spirits of three military men; who judging Dante, from his dress, to be a countryman of theirs, entreat him to stop. He complies and speaks with them. The two Poets then reach the place where the water descends, being the termination of this third compartment in the seventh circle; and here Virgil having thrown down into the hollow a cord, where-with Dante was girt, they behold at that signal a monstrous and horrible figure come swimming up to them.

CONTENTS

CANTO XIX

p. 109 - 114

<u>The Eighth Circle - The Third Bolgia</u>
They come to the third gulf, wherein are punished those who have been guilty of simony. These are fixed with the head downward into certain apertures, so that no more of them than the legs appear without, and on the soles of their feet are seen burning flames. Dante is taken down by his guide into the bottom of the gulf; and there finds Pope Nicholas the Fifth, whose evil deeds, together with those of other pontiffs are bitterly reprehended. Virgil then carries him up again to the arch, which affords them passage over the following gulf.

Scenes	*Lines*
The Simoniacs	*1 - 15*
The Third Bolgia	*16 - 28*
Pope Nicholas	*29 - 54*
The Third Bolgia	*55 - 64*
Pope Nicholas	*65 - 84*
The Third Bolgia	*85 - 99*
The Donation of Constantine	*100 - 107*
The Fourth Bolgia	*108 - 133*

Illustrations

The Simoniacs	*110*

CANTO XX

p. 115 - 120

<u>The Eighth Circle - Fourth Bolgia</u>
The Poet relates the punishment of such as presumed, while living, to predict future events. It is to have their faces reversed and set contrary way on their limbs, so that, being deprived of the power to see before them, they are constrained ever to walk backward. Among these Virgil points out to him Amphiaraüs, Tiresias, Aruns, and Manto (from the mention of whom he takes occasion to speak of the origins of Mantua), together with several others, who had practiced the arts of divination and astrology.

Scenes	*Lines*
The Diviners	*1 - 12*
The Fourth Bolgia	*13 - 30*
Tiresias and Aruns	*31 - 54*
The Fourth Bolgia	*55 - 75*
Manto	*76 - 96*
The Fourth Bolgia	*97 - 115*
Michael Scott	*116 - 126*
The Fourth Bolgia	*127 - 130*

Illustrations

Diviners and Sorcerers	*116*

CANTO XXIII

<u>The Eighth Circle - The Sixth Bolgia</u>
The enraged Demons pursue Dante, but he is preserved from them by Virgil. On reaching the sixth gulf, he beholds the punishment of the hypocrites; which is, to pace continually round the gulf under the pressure of the caps and hoods, that are gilt on the outside, but leaden within. He is addressed by two of these, Catalano and Loderingo, knights of Saint Mary, otherwise called Joyous Friars of Bologna. Caiaphas is seen fixed to a cross on the ground and he's so starched along the way, that all tread on him in passing.

CANTO XXIV

<u>The Eighth Circle - The Seventh Bolgia</u>
Under the escort of his faithful master, Dante not without difficulty makes his way out the sixth gulf; and in the seventh, sees the robbers tormented by venomous and pestilent serpents. The soul of Vanni Fucci, who had pillaged the sacristy of Saint James in Pistoia, predicts some calamities that impended over that city, and over the Florentines.

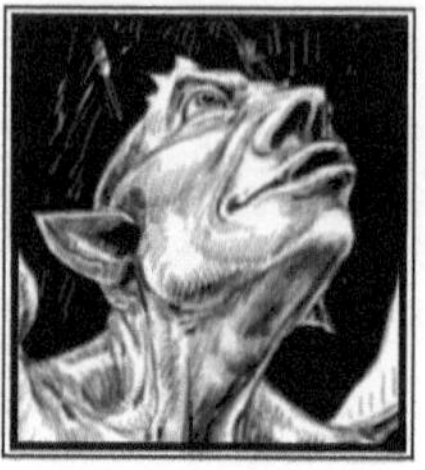

CONTENTS

CONTENTS xxvii

INTRODUCTION

ANNA TAMBOUR

To go to Hell as a tourist, guided by not only *the* expert but one you look up to with no jealousy, as he's too dead to threaten your own art—who wouldn't wish this, if the tour is a round trip.

Dante did, and in so doing, created something greater than menus as the reason many have learned Italian.

In the first line, Dante Alighieri gives us the most obvious reason he took this trip: middle-age angst. But this was far from all. His life was total turmoil. Florence in the 1300s resembled our world today. Government was so unstable yet overwhelming that it was impossible to just live your life. Powerful, self-centred factions took over the body politic; and every aspect of life took on political nuances.

Even this professional writer, Dante, as we call him as if we know him, was split between writing about (in Latin, because these were high-culture topics) the nuances of language differences, the best form of verse; and trying to survive in the deadly world of politics.

For he wrote this comedy that isn't, as an exile, having only recently been the top official in Florence's mountainous government. Accused of corruption, he was damned, and damned unsafe. Though no one now has to know the details of the personalities he throws into the circles of Hell, the Inferno is teeming with them, especially the avaricious who he condemns as only a writer can.

At the same time, he was going through not only a lovelife replete with high-medieval pining and too much pure love, but a crisis of artistic confidence so great that, to write this poetic epic, he jilted his previous favorite verse form and created a fiendishly difficult one that has bedevilled interpreters ever since. A year after he finished this life's work, he died, having created what has turned out to be many others' life's work—to republish, elaborate upon, interpret, and illustrate a tale he had titled simply *Comedia*.

The title itself is a mislead. It was originally *Comedia* in the Tuscan vernacular, which is what the poem was written in (in his treatise on language, this is one of the 14 Italian dialects he was the first to identify).

Comedia just indicated its genre—a story that ends well, as opposed to the *canzone*, a lyric mode of poetry heavy enough to handle high road topics: heroism, love, virtue—written for those who love their stories to end badly. Dante did have interesting loves, but suffered conflicts. He was greatly attracted by Bertrand de Born, whose great love was bloody war. Dante put this poet in the 8th circle of Hell, but I think only for propriety's sake.

Dante chose the Roman poet Publius Vergilius Maro, who we know as Virgil, as his guide through Hell and Purgatory, Virgil having written the definitive guide to the Underworld in his own epic poem, the *Aeneid*.

Virgil's Underworld was pre-Christian, with no real appreciation of the exquisite variations of sin, so his Underworld was a messy lot compared to Dante's, whose Hell is as neatly organised as a file structure.

Dante was a God-loving, Pope-loving Christian. He was also, not just interested in the latest scientific knowledge. Dante's journey to the center of the earth is a more science-based science fiction story than Verne's.

Numbers also play a role. They were not only symbolic in Roman times, but in medieval. But like the beasts in the epic, which are also symbolic, though it's been argued about precisely what each symbolises, you as a reader can drop down into the world of the Inferno and relate to it in your own way.

In fact, going to Hell without any commentary can be a joy. The form of *Comedia* was a change altogether for Dante. Not only was it hellishly complex, a new form of poetry, but it was mathematically complex. And though it was against sin and for a vengeful God, and thus very religious and pious and all, it was not only transparently snarky to his contemporaries (one reason that he wrote it in the Tuscan vernacular) that subsequent glosses and footnotes always weighed down his book till they've sunk most readers' interest. That's our loss. Of those who learnt Italian (Tuscan, slightly modified, became what we know as Italian) to be able to read this. Clive James, the humorist, learnt Italian to make his translation his life's work. William Blake didn't paint his watercolor illustrations until he'd learned Italian, though he had a perfectly good and recent translation he could have depended upon.

In all cases of translation and presentation, the problem is a special kind of Hell: Follow the poetry strictures, or the meaning of the words themselves, or the meaning behind the words, or the musical flow, or—and be criticised, and the hell with you, no matter which road you take. And those thorns are cotton wool compared to the blades of numbers, so important to the structure that Dante could have taught kabbalists to code.

That didn't stop a surprising lot, including poets such as Longfellow.

Dorothy Sayers considered her translation her best work.

Byron tried but gave up, the job interfering too much with the work of being infamous.

James Romanes Sibbald a Scott, first published his in 1884. It contains none of the painful double jointed language that infects so many others.

There are many translators who, going for the good stuff, only translated *The Inferno*.

This translation is one.

As for illustrators, there is one above all whose name stands out. He was an adept cartoonist, a special skill that is the reason his exquisite engravings are so telling, they have, made the epic poem into a graphic novel. Gustave Doré started with *The Inferno*, and went on, after its rave success, to illustrate the whole *Comedy*, winning a fancy prize.

Prize be damned, what Doré achieved was immortality, too late to cry for joy. For his use of black was considered gloomy by the end of his project, and soon he was as passé as the last salon.

Now that black has come into its own again, his use of light and dark in his meticulous monochromes is appreciated as he could only have wished, and *The Divine Comedy* itself is enjoyed chiefly, as his art.

I doubt, however, that these engravings would have captured Dante's jealous, retributive heart.

The man himself acted like God as a critic, consigning the Florentine artist Cimabue to Purgatory, supposedly for his arrogance, so Doré was fortunate not to be immortalised by Dante.

I think Dante would have placed both artists of this edition in a place they would have loathed. Filled with the overexposure of heavenly light, they could not even warm their hands on hot air seeping up from the Inferno.

Jim Agpalza's cover features in brilliant, Florentine blue, a beast Dante was lucky to not be a part of. Agpalza's internal illustrations take off from the starting block of Doré, and go beyond. His monochromes have a cleanliness and crispness to them, as opposed to the muddiness of Dore's currency-quality engravings, that could also have warmed Dante's heart, and does, mine. His style is at once, contemporary with Dante and our time.

But enough of this. It's time to go. *Buon viaggio.*

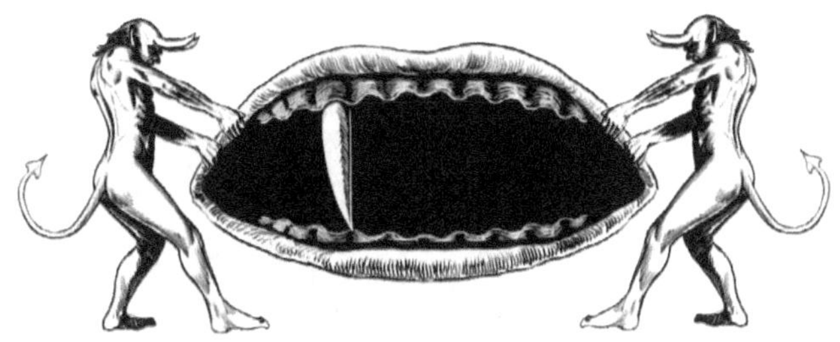

IN MIDDLE OF THE JOURNEY of our days
    I found that I was in a darksome wood—
    The right road lost and vanished in the maze.
Ah me ! how hard to make it understood
    How rough that wood was, wild, and terrible :
    By the mere thought my terror is renewed.
More bitter scarce were death.   But ere I tell
    At large of good which there by me was found,
    I will relate what other things befell.
Scarce know I how I entered on that ground,   10
    So deeply, at the moment when I passed
    From the right way, was I in slumber drowned.
But when beneath a hill arrived at last,
    Which for the boundary of the valley stood,
    That with such terror had my heart harassed,
I upwards looked and saw its shoulders glowed,
    Radiant already with that planet's light
    Which guideth surely upon every road.
A little then was quieted by the sight
    The fear which deep within my heart had lain   20
    Through all my sore experience of the night.
And as the man, who, breathing short in pain,
    Hath 'scaped the sea and struggled to the shore,
    Turns back to gaze upon the perilous main ;
Even so my soul which fear still forward bore
    Turned to review the pass whence I egressed,
    And which none, living, ever left before.
My wearied frame refreshed with scanty rest,
    I to ascend the lonely hill essayed ;
    The lower foot still that on which I pressed.   30

I

THE LEOPARD
Canto I, lines 31 - 34

And lo ! Ere I had well beginning made,
　　A nimble leopard, light upon her feet,
　　And in a skin all spotted o'er arrayed :
Nor ceased she e'er me full in the face to meet,
　　And to me in my path such hindrance threw
　　That many a time I wheeled me to retreat.
It was the hour of dawn ; with retinue
　　Of stars that were with him when Love Divine
　　In the beginning into motion drew

THE LION
Canto I, lines 35 - 45

Those beauteous things, the sun began to shine ;   40
    And I took heart to be of better cheer
    Touching the creature with the gaudy skin,
Seeing 'twas morn, and spring-tide of the year ;
    Yet not so much but that when into sight
    A lion came, I was disturbed with fear.
Towards me he seemed advancing in his might,
    Rabid with hunger and with head high thrown :
    The very air was tremulous with fright.

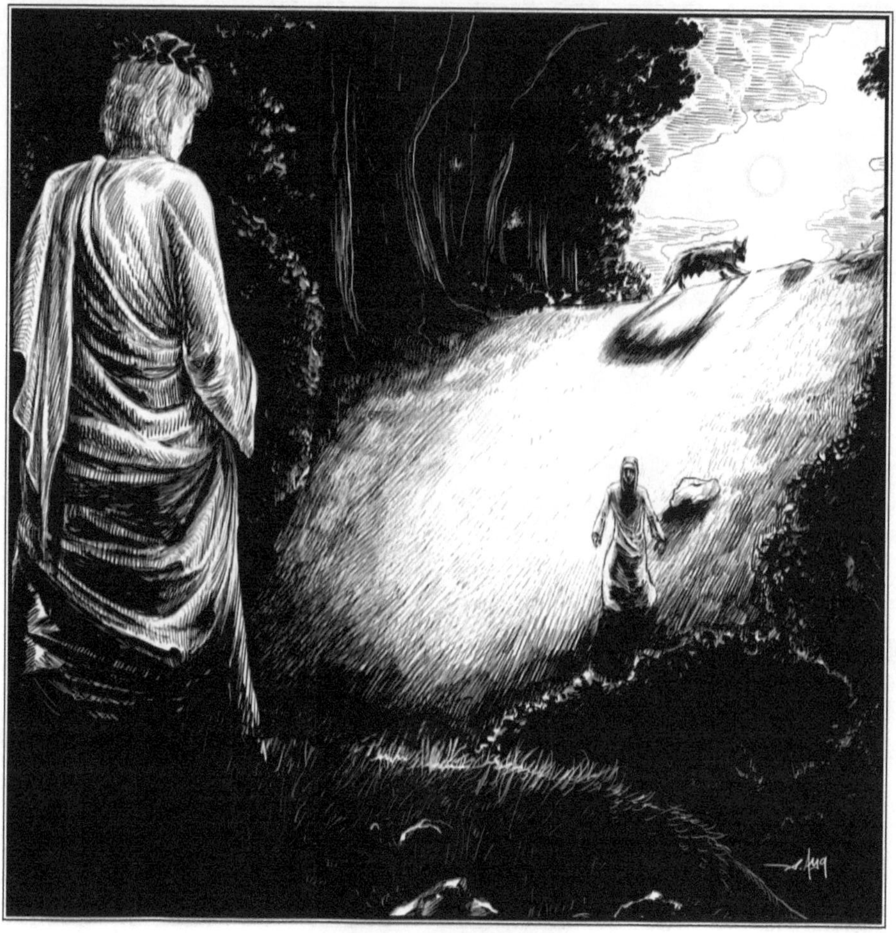

A she-wolf, too, beheld I further on ;
  All kinds of lust seemed in her leanness pent :   50
  Through her, ere now, much folk have misery known.
By her oppressed, and altogether spent
  By the terror breathing from her aspect fell,
  I lost all hope of making the ascent.
And as the man who joys while thriving well,
  When comes the time to lose what he has won
  In all his thoughts weeps inconsolable,

So mourned I through the brute which rest knows none :
    She barred my way again and yet again,
      And thrust me back where silent is the sun.   60
And as I downward rushed to reach the plain,
    Before mine eyes appeared there one aghast,
      And dumb like those that silence long maintain.
When I beheld him in the desert vast,
    ' Whate'er thou art, or ghost or man,' I cried,
      ' I pray thee show such pity as thou hast. '
' No man, though once I was ; on either side
    Lombard my parents were, and both of them
      For native place had Mantua,' he replied.
' Though late, *sub Julio*, to the world I came,   70
    And lived at Rome in good Augustus' day,
      While yet false gods and lying were supreme.
Poet I was, renowning in my lay
    Anchises' righteous son, who fled from Troy
      What time proud Ilion was to flames a prey.
But thou, why going back to such annoy ?
    The hill delectable why fear to mount,
      The origin and ground of every joy ?'
' And thou in sooth art Virgil, and the fount
    Whence in a stream so full doth language flow ?'   80
      Abashed, I answered him with humble front.
' Of other poets light and honour thou !
    Let the long study and great zeal I've shown
      In searching well thy book, avail me now !
My master thou, and author thou, alone !
    From thee alone I, borrowing, could attain
      The style consummate which has made me known.
Behold the beast which makes me turn again :
    Deliver me from her, illustrious Sage ;
      Because of her I tremble, pulse and vein.'   90
' Thou must attempt another pilgrimage.'
    Observing that I wept, he made reply,
      ' If from this waste thyself thou 'dst disengage.
Because the beast thou art afflicted by
    Will suffer none along her way to pass,
      But, hindering them, harasses till they die.

So vile a nature and corrupt she has,
    Her raging lust is still insatiate,
    And food but makes it fiercer than it was.
Many a creature hath she ta'en for mate,   100
    And more she'll wed until the hound comes forth
    To slay her and afflict with torment great.
He will not batten upon pelf or earth ;
    But he shall feed on valour, love, and lore ;
    Feltro and Feltro 'tween shall be his birth.
He will save humbled Italy, and restore,
    For which of old virgin Camilla died ;
    Turnus, Euryalus, Nisus, died of yore.
Her through all cities chasing far and wide,
    He at the last to Hell will thrust her down,   110
    Whence envy first unloosed her.   I decide
Therefore and judge that thou hadst best come on
    With me for guide ; and hence I'll lead thee where
    A place eternal shall to thee be shown.
There shalt thou hear the howlings of despair
    In which the ancient spirits make lament,
    All of them fain the second death to share.
Next shalt thou them behold who are content,
    Because they hope some time, though now in fire,
    To join the blessed they will win consent.   120
And if to these thou later wouldst aspire,
    A soul shall guide thee, worthier far than I ;
    When I depart thee will I leave with her.
Because the Emperor who reigns on high
    Wills not, since 'gainst His laws I did rebel,
    That to His city I bring any nigh.
O'er all the world He rules, there reigns as well ;
    There is His city and exalted seat :
    O happy whom He chooses there to dwell !'
And I to him :   ' Poet, I thee entreat,   130
    Even by that God who was to thee unknown,
    That I may 'scape this present ill, nor meet
With worse, conduct me whither thou hast shown,
    That I may see Saint Peter's gate, and those
    Whom thou reportest in such misery thrown.'
He moved away ; behind him held I close.

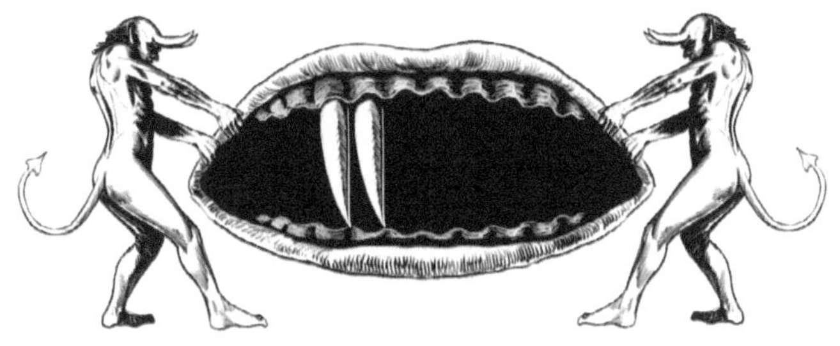

IT WAS THE CLOSE OF DAY ; the twilight brown
    All living things on earth was setting free
    From toil, while I preparing was alone
To face the battle which awaited me,
    As well of ruth as of the perilous quest,
    Now to be limned by faultless memory.
Help, lofty genius ! Muses, manifest
    Goodwill to me ! Recording what befell,
    Do thou, O mind, now show thee at thy best !
I thus began : ' Poet, and Guide as well,   10
    Ere trusting me on this adventure wide,
    Judge if my strength of it be capable.
Thou say'st that Silvius' father, ere he died,
    Still mortal to the world immortal went,
    There in the body some time to abide.
Yet that the Foe of evil was content
    That he should come, seeing what high effect,
    And who and what should from him claim descent,
No room for doubt can thoughtful man detect :
    For he of noble Rome, and of her sway   20
    Imperial, in high Heaven grew sire elect.
And both of these, the very truth to say,
    Were founded for the holy seat, whereon
    The Greater Peter's follower sits today.
Upon this journey, praised by thee, were known
    And heard things by him, to the which he owed
    His triumph, whence derives the Papal gown.
That path the Chosen Vessel later trod
    So of the faith assurance to receive,
    Which is beginning of salvation's road.   30

BEATRICE
Canto II, lines 52 - 106

But why should I go ?   Who will sanction give ?
    For I am no Æneas and no Paul ;
    Me worthy of it no one can believe,
Nor I myself.   Hence venturing at thy call,
    I dread the journey may prove rash.   But vain
    For me to reason ; wise, thou know'st it all.'
Like one no more for what he wished for fain,
    Whose purpose shares mutation with his thought
    Till from the thing begun he turns again ;
On that dim slope so grew I all distraught,   40
    Because, by brooding on it, the design
    I shrank from, which before I warmly sought.
' If well I understand these words of thine.'
    The shade of him magnanimous made reply,
    ' Thy soul 'neath cowardice hath sunk supine,
Which a man often is so burdened by,
    It makes him falter from a noble aim,
    As beasts at objects ill-distinguished shy.
To loose thee from this terror, why I came,
    And what the speech I heard, I will relate,   50
    When first of all I pitied thee.   A dame
Hailed me where I 'mongst those in dubious state
    Had my abode : so blest was she and fair,
    Her to command me I petitioned straight.
Her eyes were shining brighter than the star ;
    And she began to say in accents sweet
    And tuneable as angel's voices are :
" O Mantuan Shade, in courtesy complete,
    Whose fame survives on earth, nor less shall grow
    Through all the ages, while the world hath seat ;   60
A friend of mine, with fortune for his foe,
    Has met with hindrance on his desert way,
    And, terror-smitten, can no further go,
But turns ; and that he is too far astray,
    And that I rose too late for help, I dread,
    From what in Heaven concerning him they say.
Go, with thy speech persuasive him bestead,
    And with all needful help his guardian prove,
    That touching him I may be comforted.

Know, it is Beatrice seeks thee thus to move.   70
    Thence come I where I to return am fain :
    My coming and my plea are ruled by love.
When I shall stand before my Lord again,
    Often to Him I will renew thy praise."
    And here she ceased, nor did I dumb remain :
" O virtuous Lady, thou alone the race
    Of man exaltest 'bove all else that dwell
    Beneath the heaven which wheels in narrowest space.
To do thy bidding pleases me so well,
    Though 'twere already done 'twere all too slow ;   80
    Thy wish at greater length no need to tell.
But say, what tempted thee to come thus low,
    Even to this centre, from the region vast,
    Whither again thou art on fire to go ?"
" This much to learn since a desire thou hast,"
    She answered, " briefly thee I'll satisfy,
    How, coming here, I through no terrors passed.
We are, of right, such things alarmèd by,
    As have the power to hurt us ; all beside
    Are harmless, and not fearful.   Wherefore I—   90
Thus formed by God, His bounty is so wide—
    Am left untouched by all your miseries,
    And through this burning unmolested glide.
A noble lady is in Heaven, who sighs
    O'er the obstruction where I'd have thee go,
    And breaks the rigid edict of the skies.
Calling on Lucia, thus she made her know
    What she desired : ' Thy vassal now hath need
    Of help from thee ; do thou then helpful show.'
Lucia, who hates all cruelty, in speed   100
    Rose, and approaching where I sat at rest,
    To venerable Rachel giving heed,
Me : ' Beatrice, true praise of God,' addressed ;
    ' Why not help him who had such love for thee,
    And from the vulgar throng to win thee pressed ?
Dost thou not hear him weeping pitiably,
    Nor mark the death now threatening him upon
    A flood than which less awful is the sea ?'

Never on earth did any ever run,
      Allured by profit or impelled by fear,   110
      Swifter than I, when speaking she had done,
From sitting 'mong the blest descended here,
      My trust upon thy comely rhetoric cast,
      Which honours thee and those who lend it ear."
When of these words she spoken had the last,
      She turned aside bright eyes which tears did fill,
      And I by this was urged to greater haste.
And so it was I joined thee by her will,
      And from that raging beast delivered thee,
      Which barred the near way up the beauteous hill.   120
What ails thee then ?   Why thus a laggard be ?
      Why cherish in thy heart a craven fear ?
      Where is thy franchise, where thy bravery,
When three such blessed ladies have a care
      For thee in Heaven's court, and these words of mine
      Thee for such wealth of blessedness prepare ?'
As flowers, by chills nocturnal made to pine
      And shut themselves, when touched by morning bright
      Upon their stems arise, full-blown and fine ;
So of my faltering courage changed the plight,   130
      And such good cheer ran through my heart, it spurred
      Me to declare, like free-born generous wight :
' O pitiful, who for my succour stirred !
      And thou how full of courtesy to run,
      Alert in service, hearkening her true word !
Thou with thine eloquence my heart hast won
      To keen desire to go, and the intent
      Which first I held I now no longer shun.
Therefore proceed ; my will with thine is blent :
      Thou art my Guide, Lord, Master ; thou alone !'   140
      Thus I ; and with him, as he forward went,
The steep and rugged road I entered on.

THE GATE
Canto III, lines 1 - 15

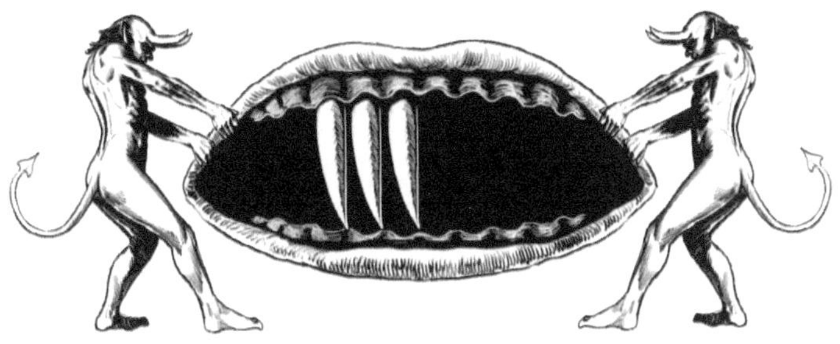

THROUGH ME TO THE CITY dolorous lies the way,
    Who pass through me shall pains eternal prove,
    Through me are reached the people lost for aye.
' Twas Justice did my Glorious Maker move ;
    I was created by the Power Divine,
    The Highest Wisdom, and the Primal Love.
No thing's creation earlier was than mine,
    If not eternal ; I for aye endure :
    Ye who make entrance, every hope resign !
These words beheld I writ in hue obscure   10
    On summit of a gateway ; wherefore I :
    ' Hard is their meaning, Master.' Like one sure
Beforehand of my thought, he made reply :
    ' Here it behoves to leave all fears behind ;
    All cowardice behoveth here to die.
For now the place I told thee of we find,
    Where thou the miserable folk shouldst see
    Who the true good of reason have resigned.'
Then, with a glance of glad serenity,
    He took my hand in his, which made me bold,   20
    And brought me in where secret things there be.
There sighs and plaints and wailings uncontrolled
    The dim and starless air resounded through ;
    Nor at the first could I from tears withhold.
The various languages and words of woe,
    The uncouth accents, mixed with angry cries
    And smiting palms and voices loud and low,
Composed a tumult which doth circling rise
    For ever in that air obscured for aye ;
    As when the sand upon the whirlwind flies.   30

THE WRETCHES
Canto III, lines 64 - 69

And, horror-stricken, I began to say :
     ' Master, what sound can this be that I hear,
     And who the folk thus whelmed in misery ?'
And he replied : ' In this condition drear
     Are held the souls of that inglorious crew
     Who lived unhonoured, but from guilt kept clear.
Mingled they are with caitiff angels, who,
     Though from avowed rebellion they refrained,
     Disloyal to God, did selfish ends pursue.
Heaven hurled them forth, lest they her beauty stained ;   40
     Received they are not by the nether hell,
     Else triumph thence were by the guilty gained.'
And I : ' What bear they, Master, to compel
     Their lamentations in such grievous tone ?'
     He answered :   ' In few words I will thee tell.
No hope of death is to the wretches known ;
     So dim the life and abject where they sigh
     They count all sufferings easier than their own.
Of them the world endures no memory ;
     Mercy and justice them alike disdain.   50
     Speak we not of them : glance, and pass them by.'
I saw a banner when I looked again,
     Which, always whirling round, advanced in haste
     As if despising steadfast to remain.
And after it so many people chased
     In long procession, I should not have said
     That death had ever wrought such countless waste.
Some first I recognised, and then the shade
     I saw and knew of him, the search to close,
     Whose dastard soul the great refusal made.   60
Straightway I knew and was assured that those
     Were of the tribe of caitiffs, even the race
     Despised of God and hated of His foes.
The wretches, who when living showed no trace
     Of life, went naked, and were fiercely stung
     By wasps and hornets swarming in that place.
Blood drawn by these out of their faces sprung
     And, mingled with their tears, was at their feet
     Sucked up by loathsome worms it fell among.

THE INFERNO

CHARON
Canto III, lines 73 - 91

Casting mine eyes beyond, of these replete,   70
      People I saw beside an ample stream,
    Whereon I said :   ' O Master, I entreat,
Tell who these are, and by what law they seem
      Impatient till across the river gone ;
    As I distinguish by this feeble gleam.'
And he :   ' These things shall unto thee be known
      What time our footsteps shall at rest be found
    Upon the woful shores of Acheron.'
Then with ashamèd eyes cast on the ground,
      Fearing my words were irksome in his ear,   80
    Until we reached the stream I made no sound.
And toward us, lo, within a bark drew near
      A veteran who with ancient hair was white,
    Shouting :   ' Ye souls depraved, be filled with fear.
Hope never more of Heaven to win the sight ;
      I come to take you to the other strand,
    To frost and fire and everlasting night.
And thou, O living soul, who there dost stand,
      From 'mong the dead withdraw thee.'   Then, aware
    That not at all I stirred at his command,   90
' By other ways, from other ports thou'lt fare ;
      But they will lead thee to another shore,
    And 'tis a skiff more buoyant must thee bear.'
And then my leader :   ' Charon, be not sore,
      For thus it has been willed where power ne'er came
    Short of the will ;   thou therefore ask no more.'
And here upon his shaggy cheeks grew tame
      Who is the pilot of the livid pool,
    And round about whose eyes glowed wheels of flame.
But all the shades, naked and spent with dool,   100
      Stood chattering with their teeth, and changing hue
    Soon as they heard the words unmerciful.
God they blasphemed, and families whence they grew ;
      Mankind, the time, place, seed in which began
    Their lives, and seed whence they were born. Then drew
They crowding all together, as they ran,
      Bitterly weeping, to the accursed shore
    Predestinate for every godless man.

The demon Charon, with eyes evermore
  Aglow, makes signals, gathering them all ;   110
  And whoso lingers smiteth with his oar.
And as the faded leaves of autumn fall
  One after the other, till at last the bough
  Sees on the ground spread all its coronal ;
With Adam's evil seed so haps it now :
  At signs each falls in turn from off the coast,
  As fowls into the ambush fluttering go.
The gloomy waters thus by them are crossed,
  And ere upon the further side they land,
  On this, anew, is gathering a host.   120
' Son,' said the courteous Master, ' understand,
  All such as in the wrath of God expire,
  From every country muster on this strand.
To cross the river they are all on fire ;
  Their wills by Heavenly justice goaded on
  Until their terror merges in desire.
This way no righteous soul has ever gone ;
  Wherefore of thee if Charon should complain,
  Now art thou sure what by his words is shown.'
When he had uttered this the dismal plain   130
  Trembled so violently, my terror past
  Recalling now, I'm bathed in sweat again.
Out of the tearful ground there moaned a blast
  Whence lightning flashed forth red and terrible,
  Which vanquished all my senses ; and, as cast
In sudden slumber, to the ground I fell.

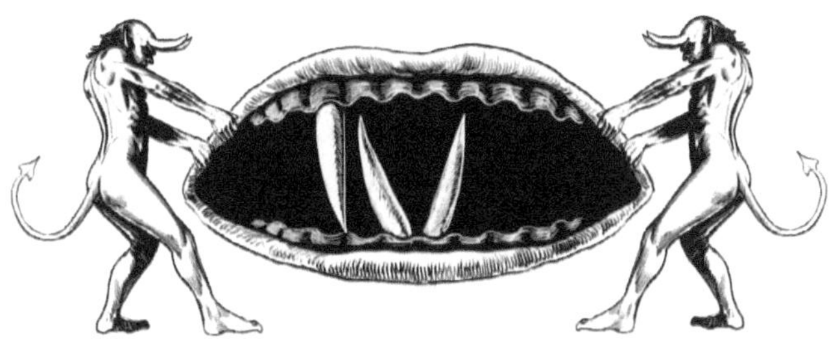

RESOUNDING THUNDER BROKE the slumber deep
    That drowsed my senses, and myself I shook
    Like one by force awakened out of sleep.
Then rising up I cast a steady look,
    With eyes refreshed, on all that lay around,
    And cognisance of where I found me took.
In sooth, me on the valley's brink I found
    Of the dolorous abyss, where infinite
    Despairing cries converge with thundering sound.
Cloudy it was, and deep, and dark as night ;   10
    So dark that, peering eagerly to find
    What its depths held, no object met my sight.
' Descend we now into this region blind.'
    Began the Poet with a face all pale ;
    ' I will go first, and do thou come behind.'
Marking the wanness on his cheek prevail,
    I asked, ' How can I, seeing thou hast dread,
    My wonted comforter when doubts assail ?'
' The anguish of the people,' then he said,
    ' Who are below, has painted on my face   20
    Pity, by thee for fear interpreted.
Come ! The long journey bids us move apace.'
    Then entered he and made me enter too
    The topmost circle girding the abyss.
Therein, as far as I by listening knew,
    There was no lamentation save of sighs,
    Whence throbbed the air eternal through and through.
This, sorrow without suffering made arise
    From infants and from women and from men,
    Gathered in great and many companies.   30

And the good Master :   ' Wouldst thou nothing then
        Of who those spirits are have me relate ?
        Yet know, ere passing further, although when
On earth they sinned not, worth however great
        Availed them not, they being unbaptized—
        Part of the faith thou holdest.   If their fate
Was to be born ere man was Christianised,
        God, as behoved, they never could adore :
        And I myself am with this folk comprised.
For such defects—our guilt is nothing more—   40
        We are thus lost, suffering from this alone
        That, hopeless, we our want of bliss deplore.'
Greatly I sorrowed when he made this known,
        Because I knew that some who did excel
        In worthiness were to that limbo gone.
' Tell me, O Sir,' I prayed him, ' Master, tell.'
        —That I of the belief might surety win,
        Victorious every error to dispel—
' Did ever any hence to bliss attain
        By merit of another or his own ?'   50
        And he, to whom my hidden drift was plain :
' I to this place but lately had come down,
        When I beheld one hither make descent ;
        A Potentate who wore a victor's crown.
The shade of our first sire forth with him went,
        And his son Abel's, Noah's forth he drew,
        Moses' who gave the laws, the obedient
Patriarch Abram's, and King David's too ;
        And, with his sire and children, Israel,
        And Rachel, winning whom such toils he knew ;   60
And many more, in blessedness to dwell.
        And I would have thee know, earlier than these
        No human soul was ever saved from Hell.'
While thus he spake our progress did not cease,
        But we continued through the wood to stray ;
        The wood, I mean, with crowded ghosts for trees.
Ere from the summit far upon our way
        We yet had gone, I saw a flame which glowed,
        Holding a hemisphere of dark at bay.

THE GREAT POETS
HOMER, HORACE, OVID, AND LUCAN
Canto IV, lines 73 - 91

'Twas still a little further on our road,   70
    Yet not so far but that in part I guessed
    That honourable people there abode.
'Of art and science Ornament confessed !
    Who are these honoured in such high degree,
    And in their lot distinguished from the rest ?'
He said : 'For them their glorious memory,
    Still in thy world the subject of renown,
    Wins grace by Heaven distinguished thus to be.'

Meanwhile I heard a voice :   ' Be honour shown
     To the illustrious poet, for his shade   80
     Is now returning which a while was gone.'
When the voice paused nor further utterance made,
     Four mighty shades drew near with one accord,
     In aspect neither sorrowful nor glad.
' Consider that one, armèd with a sword.'
     Began my worthy Master in my ear,
     ' Before the three advancing like their lord ;
For he is Homer, poet with no peer :
     Horace the satirist is next in line,
     Ovid comes third, and Lucan in the rear.   90
And 'tis because their claim agrees with mine
     Upon the name they with one voice did cry,
     They to their honour in my praise combine.'
Thus I beheld their goodly company—
     The lords of song in that exalted style
     Which o'er all others, eagle-like, soars high.
Having conferred among themselves a while
     They turned toward me and salutation made,
     And, this beholding, did my Master smile.
And honour higher still to me was paid,   100
     For of their company they made me one ;
     So I the sixth part 'mong such genius played.
Thus journeyed we to where the brightness shone,
     Holding discourse which now 'tis well to hide,
     As, where I was, to hold it was well done.
At length we reached a noble castle's side
     Which lofty sevenfold walls encompassed round,
     And it was moated by a sparkling tide.
This we traversed as if it were dry ground ;
     I through seven gates did with those sages go ;   110
     Then in a verdant mead people we found
Whose glances were deliberate and slow.
     Authority was stamped on every face ;
     Seldom they spake, in tuneful voices low.
We drew apart to a high open space
     Upon one side which, luminously serene,
     Did of them all a perfect view embrace.

Thence, opposite, on the enamel green
    Were shown me mighty spirits ; with delight
    I still am stirred them only to have seen.   120
With many more, Electra was in sight ;
    ' Mong them I Hector and Æneas spied,
    Cæsar in arms, his eyes, like falcon's, bright.
And, opposite, Camilla I descried ;
    Penthesilea too ; the Latian King
    Sat with his child Lavinia by his side.
Brutus I saw, who Tarquin forth did fling ;
    Cornelia, Marcia, Julia, and Lucrece.
    Saladin sat alone.   Considering
What lay beyond with somewhat lifted eyes,   130
    The Master I beheld of those that know,
    ' Mong such as in philosophy were wise.
All gazed on him as if toward him to show
    Becoming honour ; Plato in advance
    With Socrates :   the others stood below.
Democritus who set the world on chance ;
    Thales, Diogenes, Empedocles,
    Zeno, and Anaxagoras met my glance ;
Heraclitus, and Dioscorides,
    Wise judge of nature.   Tully, Orpheus, were   140
    With ethic Seneca and Linus.   These,
And Ptolemy, too, and Euclid, geometer,
    Galen, Hippocrates, and Avicen,
    Averroes, the same who did prepare
The Comment, saw I ; nor can tell again
    The names of all I saw ; the subject wide
    So urgent is, time often fails me.   Then
Into two bands the six of us divide ;
    Me by another way my Leader wise
    Doth from the calm to air which trembles, guide.   150
I reach a part which all benighted lies.

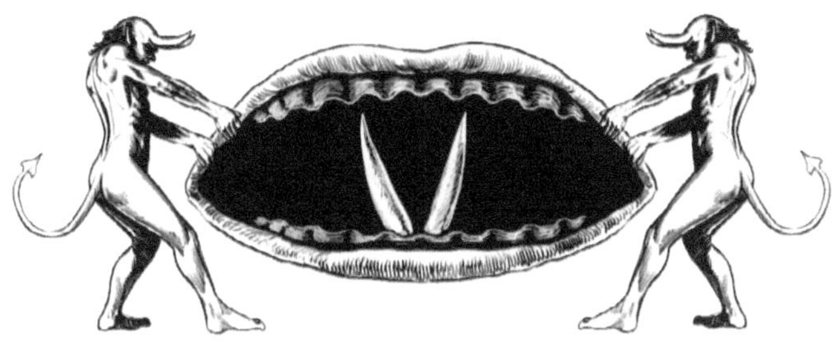

FROM THE FIRST CIRCLE thus I downward went
    Into the Second, which girds narrower space,
    But greater woe compelling loud lament.
Minos waits awful there and snarls, the case
    Examining of all who enter in ;
    And, as he girds him, dooms them to their place.
I say, each ill-starred spirit must begin
    On reaching him its guilt in full to tell ;
    And he, omniscient as concerning sin,
Sees to what circle it belongs in Hell ;   10
    Then round him is his tail as often curled
    As he would have it stages deep to dwell.
And evermore before him stand a world
    Of shades ; and all in turn to judgment come,
    Confess and hear, and then are downward hurled.
' O thou who comest to the very home
    Of woe,' when he beheld me Minos cried,
    Ceasing a while from utterance of doom,
' Enter not rashly nor in all confide ;
    By ease of entering be not led astray.'   20
    ' Why also growling ?' answered him my Guide ;
' Seek not his course predestinate to stay ;
    For thus 'tis willed where nothing ever fails
    Of what is willed.   No further speech essay.'
And now by me are agonising wails
    Distinguished plain ; now am I come outright
    Where grievous lamentation me assails.
Now had I reached a place devoid of light,
    Raging as in a tempest howls the sea
    When with it winds, blown thwart each other, fight.   30

THE INFERNO

MINOS AND THE TEMPEST
Canto V, lines 1 - 36

The infernal storm is raging ceaselessly,
    Sweeping the shades along with it, and them
    It smites and whirls, nor lets them ever be.
Arrived at the precipitous extreme,
    In shrieks and lamentations they complain,
    And even the Power Divine itself blaspheme.
I understood that to this mode of pain
    Are doomed the sinners of the carnal kind,
    Who o'er their reason let their impulse reign.
As starlings in the winter-time combined   40
    Float on the wing in crowded phalanx wide,
    So these bad spirits, driven by that wind,
Float up and down and veer from side to side ;
    Nor for their comfort any hope they spy
    Of rest, or even of suffering mollified.
And as the cranes in long-drawn company
    Pursue their flight while uttering their song,
    So I beheld approach with wailing cry
Shades lifted onward by that whirlwind strong.
    ' Master, what folk are these,' I therefore said,   50
    ' Who by the murky air are whipped along ?'
' She, first of them,' his answer thus was made,
    ' Of whom thou wouldst a wider knowledge win,
    O'er many tongues and peoples, empire swayed.
So ruined was she by licentious sin
    That she decreed lust should be uncontrolled,
    To ease the shame that she herself was in.
She is Semiramis, of whom 'tis told
    She followed Ninus, and his wife had been.
    Hers were the realms now by the Sultan ruled.   60
The next is she who, amorous and self-slain,
    Unto Sichæus' dust did faithless show :
    Then lustful Cleopatra.'   Next was seen
Helen, for whom so many years in woe
    Ran out ; and I the great Achilles knew,
    Who at the last encountered love for foe.
Paris I saw and Tristram.   In review
    A thousand shades and more, he one by one
    Pointed and named, whom love from life withdrew.

And after I had heard my Teacher run   70
    O'er many a dame of yore and many a knight,
    I, lost in pity, was well nigh undone.
Then I :　'O Poet, if I only might
    Speak with the two that as companions hie,
    And on the wind appear to be so light !'
And he to me :　'When they shall come more nigh
    Them shalt thou mark, and by the love shalt pray
    Which leads them onward, and they will comply.'
Soon as the wind bends them to where we stay
    I lift my voice :　'O wearied souls and worn !   80
    Come speak with us if none the boon gainsay.'
Then even as doves,urged by desire, return
    On outspread wings and firm to their sweet nest
    As through the air by mere volition borne,
From Dido's band those spirits issuing pressed
    Towards where we were, athwart the air malign ;
    My passionate prayer such influence possessed.
'O living creature, gracious and benign,
    Us visiting in this obscurèd air,
    Who did the earth with blood incarnadine ;   90
If in the favour of the King we were
    Who rules the world, we for thy peace would pray,
    Since our misfortunes thy compassion stir.
Whate'er now pleases thee to hear or say
    We listen to, or tell, at your demand ;
    While yet the wind, as now, doth silent stay.
My native city lies upon the strand
    Where to the sea descends the river Po
    For peace, with all his tributary band.
Love, in a generous heart set soon aglow,   100
    Seized him for the fair form was mine above ;
    And still it irks me to have lost it so.
Love, which absolves no one beloved from love,
    So strong a passion for him in me wrought
    That, as thou seest, I still its mastery prove.
Love led us where we in one death were caught.
    For him who slew us waits Caïna now.'
    Unto our ears these words from them were brought.

When I had heard these troubled souls, my brow
    I downward bent, and long while musing stayed,   110
    Until the Poet asked : ' What thinkest thou ?'
And when I answered him, ' Alas !' I said,
    ' Sweet thoughts how many, and what strong desire,
    These to their sad catastrophe betrayed !'
Then, turned once more to them, I to inquire
    Began : ' Francesca, these thine agonies
    Me with compassion unto tears inspire.
But tell me, at the season of sweet sighs
    What sign made love, and what the means he chose
    To strip your dubious longings of disguise ?'   120
And she to me : ' The bitterest of woes
    Is to remember in the midst of pain
    A happy past ; as well thy teacher knows.
Yet none the less, and since thou art so fain
    The first occasion of our love to hear,
    Like one I speak that cannot tears restrain.
As we for pastime one day reading were
    How Lancelot by love was fettered fast—
    All by ourselves and without any fear—
Moved by the tale our eyes we often cast   130
    On one another, and our colour fled ;
    But one word was it, vanquished us at last.
When how the smile, long wearied for, we read
    Was kissed by him who loved like none before,
    This one, who henceforth never leaves me, laid
A kiss on my mouth, trembling the while all o'er.
    The book was Galahad, and he as well
    Who wrote the book.   That day we read no more.'
And while one shade continued thus to tell,
    The other wept so bitterly, I swooned   140
    Away for pity, and as dead I fell :
Yea, as a corpse falls, fell I on the ground.

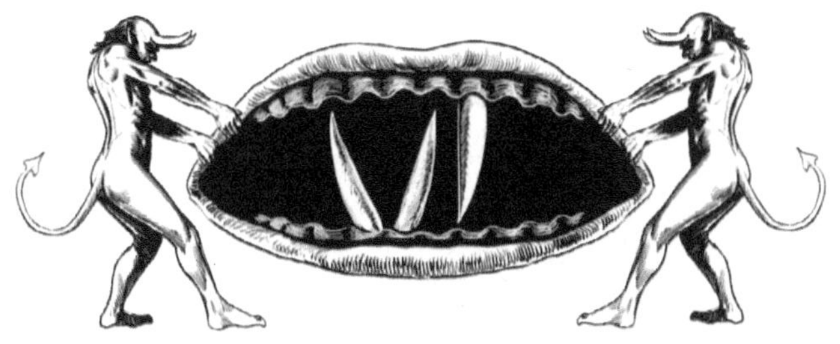

WHEN I REGAINED MY SENSES, which had fled
    At my compassion for the kindred two,
    Which for pure sorrow quite had turned my head,
New torments and a crowd of sufferers new
    I see around me as I move again,
    Where'er I turn, where'er I bend my view.
In the Third Circle am I of the rain
    Which, heavy, cold, eternal, big with woe,
    Doth always of one kind and force remain.
Large hail and turbid water, mixed with snow,   10
    Keep pouring down athwart the murky air ;
    And from the ground they fall on, stenches grow.
The savage Cerberus, a monster drear,
    Howls from his threefold throat with canine cries
    Above the people who are whelmèd there.
Oily and black his beard, and red his eyes,
    His belly huge : claws from his fingers sprout.
    The shades he flays, hooks, rends in cruel wise.
Beat by the rain these, dog-like, yelp and shout,
    And shield themselves in turn with either side ;   20
    And oft the wretched sinners turn about.
When we by Cerberus, great worm, were spied,
    He oped his mouths and all his fangs he showed,
    While not a limb did motionless abide.
My Leader having spread his hands abroad,
    Filled both his fists with earth ta'en from the ground,
    And down the ravening gullets flung the load.
Then, as sharp set with hunger barks the hound,
    But is appeased when at his meat he gnaws,
    And, worrying it, forgets all else around ;   30

CERBERUS
Canto VI, lines 1 - 18

So with those filthy faces there it was
     Of the fiend Cerberus, who deafs the crowd
     Of souls till they from hearing fain would pause.
We, travelling o'er the spirits who lay cowed
     And sorely by the grievous showers harassed,
     Upon their semblances of bodies trod.
Prone on the ground the whole of them were cast,
     Save one of them who sat upright with speed
     When he beheld that near to him we passed.
' O thou who art through this Inferno led,   40
     Me if thou canst.' he asked me, ' recognise;
     For ere I was dismantled thou wast made.'
And I to him: ' Thy present tortured guise
     Perchance hath blurred my memory of thy face,
     Until it seems I ne'er on thee set eyes.

But tell me who thou art, within this place
    So cruel set, exposed to such a pain,
    Than which, if greater, none has more disgrace.'
And he : ' Thy city, swelling with the bane
    Of envy till the sack is running o'er,   50
    Me in the life serene did once contain.
As Ciaccome your citizens named of yore ;
    And for the damning sin of gluttony
    I, as thou seest, am beaten by this shower.
No solitary woful soul am I,
    For all of these endure the selfsame doom
    For the same fault.' Here ended his reply.
I answered him, ' O Ciacco, with such gloom
    Thy misery weighs me, I to weep am prone ;
    But, if thou canst, declare to what shall come   60
The citizens of the divided town.
    Holds it one just man ? And declare the cause
    Why 'tis of discord such a victim grown.'
Then he to me : ' After contentious pause
    Blood will be spilt ; the boorish party then
    Will chase the others forth with grievous loss.
The former it behoves to fall again
    Within three suns, the others to ascend,
    Holpen by him whose wiles ere now are plain.
Long time, with heads held high, they'll make to bend   70
    The other party under burdens dire,
    Howe'er themselves in tears and rage they spend.
There are two just men, at whom none inquire.
    Envy, and pride, and avarice, even these
    Are the three sparks have set all hearts on fire.'
With this the tearful sound he made to cease :
    And I to him, ' Yet would I have thee tell—
    And of thy speech do thou the gift increase—
Tegghiaio and Farinata, honourable,
    James Rusticucci, Mosca, Arrigo,   80
    With all the rest so studious to excel
In good ; where are they ? Help me this to know ;
    Great hunger for the news hath seizèd me ;
    Delights them Heaven, or tortures Hell below ?'

He said : ' Among the blackest souls they be ;
    Them to the bottom weighs another sin.
    Shouldst thou so far descend, thou mayst them see.
But when the sweet world thou again dost win,
    I pray thee bring me among men to mind ;
    No more I tell, nor new reply begin.'   90
Then his straightforward eyes askance declined ;
    He looked at me a moment ere his head
    He bowed ; then fell flat 'mong the other blind.
' Henceforth he waketh not,' my Leader said,
    ' Till he shall hear the angel's trumpet sound,
    Ushering the hostile Judge.   By every shade
Its dismal sepulchre shall then be found,
    Its flesh and ancient form it shall resume,
    And list what echoes in eternal round.'
So passed we where the shades and rainy spume   100
    Made filthy mixture, with steps taken slow ;
    Touching a little on the world to come.
Wherefore I said : ' Master, shall torments grow
    After the awful sentence hath been heard,
    Or lesser prove and not so fiercely glow ?'
' Repair unto thy Science,' was his word ;
    ' Which tells, as things approach a perfect state
    To keener joy or suffering they are stirred.
Therefore although this people cursed by fate
    Ne'er find perfection in its full extent,   110
    To it they then shall more approximate
Than now.   ' Our course we round the circle bent,
    Still holding speech, of which I nothing say,
    Until we came where down the pathway went :
There found we Plutus, the great enemy.

PLUTUS

Canto VI, lines 110 - 115
Canto VII, lines 1 - 13

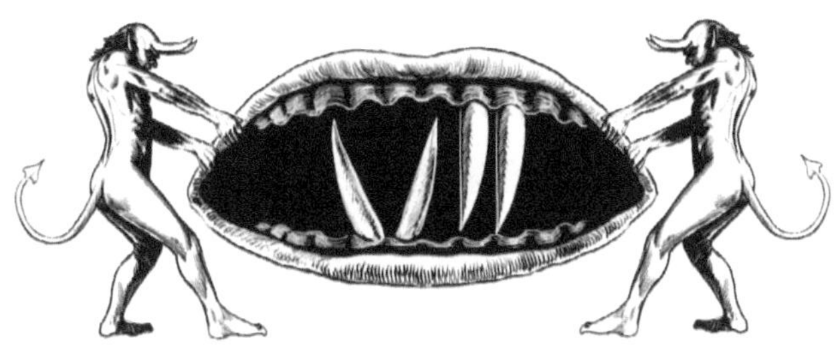

PAPE SATAN ! PAPE SATAN ! ALEPPE !
    Plutus began in accents rough and hard :
    And that mild Sage, all-knowing, said to me,
For my encouragement :   'Pay no regard
    Unto thy fear ; whatever power he sways
    Thy passage down this cliff shall not be barred.'
Then turning round to that inflamèd face
    He bade :   'Accursed wolf, at peace remain ;
    And, pent within thee, let thy fury blaze.
Down to the pit we journey not in vain :   10
    So rule they where by Michael in Heaven's height
    On the adulterous pride was vengeance ta'en.'
Then as the bellied sails, by wind swelled tight,
    Suddenly drag whenever snaps the mast ;
    Such, falling to the ground, the monster's plight.
To the Fourth Cavern so we downward passed,
    Winning new reaches of the doleful shore
    Where all the vileness of the world is cast.
Justice of God ! which pilest more and more
    Pain as I saw, and travail manifold !   20
    Why will we sin, to be thus wasted sore ?
As at Charybdis waves are forward rolled
    To break on other billows midway met,
    The people here a counter dance must hold.
A greater crowd than I had seen as yet,
    With piercing yells advanced on either track,
    Rolling great stones to which their chests were set.
They crashed together, and then each turned back
    Upon the way he came, while shouts arise,
    'Why clutch it so ?' And 'Why to hold it slack ?'   30

MISERS AND SPENDTHRIFTS
Canto VII, lines 14 - 54

In the dark circle wheeled they on this wise
    From either hand to the opposing part,
    Where evermore they raised insulting cries.
Thither arrived, each, turning, made fresh start
    Through the half circle a new joust to run ;
    And I, stung almost to the very heart,
Said, ' O my Master, wilt thou make it known
    Who the folk are ?   Were these all clerks who go
    Before us on the left, with shaven crown ?'
And he replied :   ' All of them squinted so   40
    In mental vision while in life they were,
    They nothing spent by rule.   And this they show,
And with their yelping voices make appear
    When half-way round the circle they have sped,
    And sins opposing them asunder tear.
Each wanting thatch of hair upon his head
    Was once a clerk, or pope, or cardinal,
    In whom abound the ripest growths of greed.'
And I :   ' O Master, surely among all
    Of these I ought some few to recognise,   50
    Who by such filthy sins were held in thrall.'
And he to me :   ' Vain thoughts within thee rise ;
    Their witless life, which made them vile, now mocks—
    Dimming their faces still—all searching eyes.
Eternally they meet with hostile shocks ;
    These rising from the tomb at last shall stand
    With tight clenched fists, and those with ruined locks.
Squandering or hoarding, they the happy land
    Have lost, and now are marshalled for this fray ;
    Which to describe doth no fine words demand.   60
Know hence, my Son, how fleeting is the play
    Of goods at the dispose of Fortune thrown,
    And which mankind to such fierce strife betray.
Not all the gold which is beneath the moon
    Could purchase peace, nor all that ever was,
    To but one soul of these by toil undone.'
' Master,' I said, ' tell thou, ere making pause,
    Who Fortune is of whom thou speak'st askance,
    Who holds all worldly riches in her claws.'

' O foolish creatures, lost in ignorance !'   70
    He answer made.   ' Now see that the reply
    Thou store, which I concerning her advance.
He who in knowledge is exalted high,
    Framing all Heavens gave such as should them guide,
    That so each part might shine to all ; whereby
Is equal light diffused on every side :
    And likewise to one guide and governor,
    Of worldly splendours did control confide,
That she in turns should different peoples dower
    With this vain good ; from blood should make it pass   80
    To blood, in spite of human wit.   Hence, power,
Some races failing, other some amass,
    According to her absolute decree
    Which hidden lurks, like serpent in the grass.
Vain 'gainst her foresight yours must ever be.
    She makes provision, judges, holds her reign,
    As doth his power supreme each deity.
Her permutations can no truce sustain ;
    Necessity compels her to be swift,
    So swift they follow who their turn must gain.   90
And this is she whom they so often lift
    Upon the cross, who ought to yield her praise ;
    And blame on her and scorn unjustly shift.
But she is blest nor hears what any says,
    With other primal creatures turns her sphere,
    Jocund and glad, rejoicing in her ways.
To greater woe now let us downward steer.
    The stars which rose when I began to guide
    Are falling now, nor may we linger here.'
We crossed the circle to the other side,   100
    Arriving where a boiling fountain fell
    Into a brooklet by its streams supplied.
In depth of hue the flood did perse excel,
    And we, with this dim stream to lead us on,
    Descended by a pathway terrible.
A marsh which by the name of Styx is known,
    Fed by this gloomy brook, lies at the base
    Of threatening cliffs hewn out of cold grey stone.

THE WRATHFUL
Canto VII, lines 116 - 130

And I, intent on study of the place,
>Saw people in that ditch, mud-smeared.   In it   110
>All naked stood with anger-clouded face.
Nor with their fists alone each fiercely hit
>The other, but with feet and chest and head,
>And with their teeth to shreds each other bit.
' Son, now behold,' the worthy Master said,
>' The souls of those whom anger made a prize ;
>And, further, I would have thee certified
That 'neath the water people utter sighs,
>And make the bubbles to the surface come ;
>As thou mayst see by casting round thine eyes.   120
Fixed in the mud they say :   " We lived in gloom
>In the sweet air made jocund by the day,
>Nursing within us melancholy fume.
In this black mud we now our gloom display."
>This hymn with gurgling throats they strive to sound,
>Which they in speech unbroken fail to say.'
And thus about the loathsome pool we wound
>For a wide arc, between the dry and soft,
>With eyes on those who gulp the filth, turned round.
At last we reached a tower that soared aloft.   130

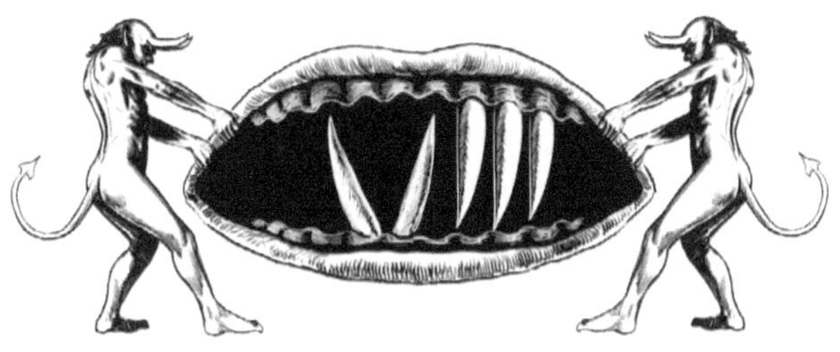

I SAY, CONTINUING, that long before
    To its foundations we approachèd nigh
    Our eyes went travelling to the top of the tower ;
For, hung out there, two flames we could espy.
    Then at such distance, scarce our eyesight made
    It clearly out, another gave reply.
And, to the Sea of Knowledge turned, I said :
    ' What meaneth this ? And what reply would yield
    That other light, and who have it displayed ?'
' Thou shouldst upon the impure watery field.'   10
    He said, ' already what approaches know,
    But that the fen-fog holds it still concealed.'
Never was arrow yet from sharp-drawn bow
    Urged through the air upon a swifter flight
    Than what I saw a tiny vessel show,
Across the water shooting into sight ;
    A single pilot served it for a crew,
    Who shouted :   ' Art thou come, thou guilty sprite ?'
' O Phlegyas, Phlegyas, this thy loud halloo !
    For once,' my Lord said, ' idle is and vain.   20
    Thou hast us only till the mud we're through.'
And, as one cheated inly smarts with pain
    When the deceit wrought on him is betrayed,
    His gathering ire could Phlegyas scarce contain.
Into the bark my Leader stepped, and made
    Me take my place beside him ; nor a jot,
    Till I had entered, was it downward weighed.
Soon as my Guide and I were in the boat,
    To cleave the flood began the ancient prow,
    Deeper than 'tis with others wont to float.   30

PHLEGYAS
Canto VIII, lines 14 - 36

Then, as the stagnant ditch we glided through,
        One smeared with filth in front of me arose
        And said :   ‘ Thus coming ere thy period, who
Art thou ?’   And I :   ‘ As one who forthwith goes
        I come ; but thou defiled, how name they thee ?’
        ‘ I am but one who weeps,’ he said.   ‘ With woes.’
I answered him, ‘ with tears and misery,
        Accursèd soul, remain ; for thou art known
        Unto me now, all filthy though thou be.’
Then both his hands were on the vessel thrown ;   40
        But him my wary Master backward heaved,
        Saying :   ‘ Do thou ’mong the other dogs be gone !’
Then to my neck with both his arms he cleaved,
        And kissed my face, and, ‘ Soul disdainful,’ said,
        ‘ O blessed she in whom thou wast conceived !
He in the world great haughtiness displayed.
        No deeds of worth his memory adorn ;
        And therefore rages here his sinful shade.
And many are there by whom crowns are worn
        On earth, shall wallow here like swine in mire,   50
        Leaving behind them names o’erwhelmed in scorn.’
And I :   ‘ O Master, I have great desire
        To see him well soused in this filthy tide,
        Ere from the lake we finally retire.’
And he :   ‘ Or ever shall have been descried
        The shore by thee, thy longing shall be met ;
        For such a wish were justly gratified.’
A little after in such fierce onset
        The miry people down upon him bore,
        I praise and bless God for it even yet.   60
‘ Philip Argenti ! at him !’ was the roar ;
        And then that furious spirit Florentine
        Turned with his teeth upon himself and tore.
Here was he left, nor wins more words of mine.
        Now in my ears a lamentation rung,
        Whence I to search what lies ahead begin.
And the good Master told me :   ‘ Son, ere long
        We to the city called of Dis draw near,
        Where in great armies cruel burghers throng.’

And I : 'Already, Master, I appear   70
     Mosques in the valley to distinguish well,
     Vermilion, as if they from furnace were
Fresh come.'   And he :   'Fires everlasting dwell
     Within them, whence appear they glowing hot,
     As thou discernest in this lower hell.'
We to the moat profound at length were brought,
     Which girds that city all disconsolate ;
     The walls around it seemed of iron wrought.
Not without fetching first a compass great,
     We came to where with angry cry at last :   80
     'Get out,' the boatman yelled ; 'behold the gate !'
More than a thousand, who from Heaven were cast,
     I saw above the gates, who furiously
     Demanded : 'Who, ere death on him has passed,
Holds through the region of the dead his way ?'
     And my wise Master made to them a sign
     That he had something secretly to say.
Then ceased they somewhat from their great disdain,
     And said :   'Come thou, but let that one be gone
     Who thus presumptuous enters on this reign.   90
Let him retrace his madcap way alone,
     If he but can ; thou meanwhile lingering here,
     Through such dark regions who hast led him down.'
Judge, reader, if I was not filled with fear,
     Hearing the words of this accursèd threat ;
     For of return my hopes extinguished were.
'Beloved Guide, who more than seven times set
     Me in security, and safely brought
     Through frightful dangers in my progress met,
Leave me not thus undone ;' I him besought :   100
     'If further progress be to us denied,
     Let us retreat together, tarrying not.'
The Lord who led me thither then replied :
     'Fear not : by One so great has been assigned
     Our passage, vainly were all hindrance tried.
Await me here, and let thy fainting mind
     Be comforted and with good hope be fed,
     Not to be left in this low world behind.'

Thus goes he, thus am I abandonèd
    By my sweet Father.   I in doubt remain,   110
    With Yes and No contending in my head.
I could not hear what speech he did maintain,
    But no long time conferred he in that place,
    Till, to be first, all inward raced again.
And then the gates were closed in my Lord's face
    By these our enemies ; outside stood he ;
    Then backward turned to me with lingering pace,
With downcast eyes, and all the bravery
    Stripped from his brows ; and he exclaimed with sighs ;
    'Who dare deny the doleful seats to me !'   120
And then he said :   'Although my wrath arise,
    Fear not, for I to victory will pursue,
    Howe'er within they plot, the enterprise.
This arrogance of theirs is nothing new ;
    They showed it once at a less secret door
    Which stands unbolted since.   Thou didst it view,
And saw the dark-writ legend which it bore.
    Thence, even now, is one who hastens down
    Through all the circles, guideless, to this shore,
And he shall win us entrance to the town.'   130

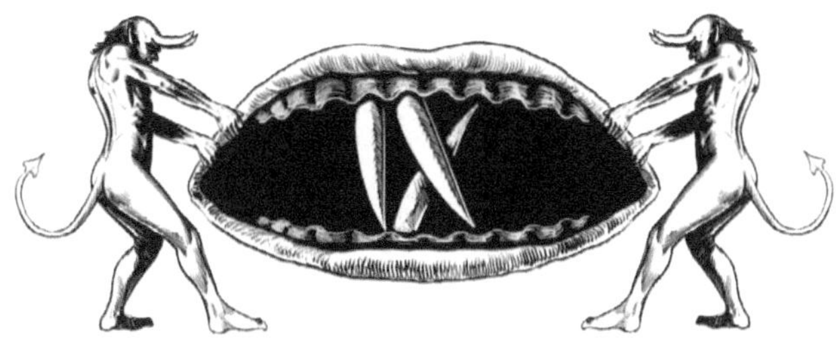

*The City of Dis, which is the Sixth Circle and that of the Heretics ❧ the Furies
and the Medusa head ❧ the Messenger of Heaven who opens the gates for
Virgil and Dante ❧ the entrance to the City ❧ the red-hot Tombs*

THE HUE WHICH cowardice on my face did paint
  When I beheld my guide return again,
  Put his new colour quicker 'neath restraint.
Like one who listens did he fixed remain ;
  For far to penetrate the air like night,
  And heavy mist, the eye was bent in vain.
' Yet surely we must vanquish in the fight ;'
  Thus he, ' unless—but with such proffered aid—
  O how I weary till he come in sight !'
Well I remarked how he transition made,   10
  Covering his opening words with those behind,
  Which contradicted what at first he said.
Nath'less his speech with terror charged my mind,
  For, haply, to the word which broken fell
  Worse meaning than he purposed, I assigned.
Down to this bottom of the dismal shell
  Comes ever any from the First Degree,
  Where all their pain is, stripped of hope to dwell ?
To this my question thus responded he :
  ' Seldom it haps to any to pursue   20
  The journey now embarked upon by me.
Yet I ere this descended, it is true,
  Beneath a spell of dire Erichtho's laid,
  Who could the corpse with soul inform anew.
Short while my flesh of me was empty made
  When she required me to o'erpass that wall,
  From Judas' circle to abstract a shade.
That is the deepest, darkest place of all,
  And furthest from the heaven which moves the skies ;
  I know the way ; fear nought that can befall.   30

THE FURIES
Canto IX, lines 35 - 61

These fens from which vile exhalations rise
    The doleful city all around invest,
    Which now we reach not save in angry wise.'
Of more he spake nought in my mind doth rest,
    For, with mine eyes, my every thought had been
    Fixed on the lofty tower with flaming crest,
Where, in a moment and upright, were seen
    Three hellish furies, all with blood defaced,
    And woman-like in members and in mien.
Hydras of brilliant green begirt their waist ;   40
    Snakes and cerastes for their tresses grew,
    And these were round their dreadful temples braced.
That they the drudges were, full well he knew,
    Of her who is the queen of endless woes,
    And said to me : ' The fierce Erynnyes view !
Herself upon the left Megæra shows ;
    That is Alecto weeping on the right ;
    Tisiphone's between.'   Here made he close.
Each with her nails her breast tore, and did smite
    Herself with open palms. They screamed in tone   50
    So fierce, I to the Poet clove for fright.
' Medusa, come, that we may make him stone !'
    All shouted as they downward gazed ; ' Alack !
    Theseus escaped us when he ventured down.'
' Keep thine eyes closed and turn to them thy back,
    For if the Gorgon chance to be displayed
    And thou shouldst look, farewell the upward track !'
Thus spake the Master, and himself he swayed
    Me round about ; nor put he trust in mine
    But his own hands upon mine eyelids laid.   60
O ye with judgment gifted to divine
    Look closely now, and mark what hidden lore
    Lies 'neath the veil of my mysterious line !
Across the turbid waters came a roar
    And crash of sound, which big with fear arose :
    Because of it fell trembling either shore.
The fashion of it was as when there blows
    A blast by cross heats made to rage amain,
    Which smites the forest and without repose

THE MESSENGER
Canto VIII, lines 62 - 91

The shattered branches sweeps in hurricane ; 70
    In clouds of dust, majestic, onward flies,
    Wild beasts and herdsmen driving o'er the plain.
' Sharpen thy gaze,' he bade—and freed mine eyes—
    ' Across the foam-flecked immemorial lake,
    Where sourest vapour most unbroken lies.'
And as the frogs before the hostile snake
    Together of the water get them clear,
    And on the dry ground, huddling, shelter take ;
More than a thousand ruined souls in fear
    Beheld I flee from one who, dry of feet, 80
    Was by the Stygian ferry drawing near.
Waving his left hand he the vapour beat
    Swiftly from 'fore his face, nor seemed he spent
    Save with fatigue at having this to meet.
Well I opined that he from Heaven was sent,
    And to my Master turned.   His gesture taught
    I should be dumb and in obeisance bent.
Ah me, how with disdain appeared he fraught !
    He reached the gate, which, touching with a rod,
    He oped with ease, for it resisted not. 90
' People despised and banished far from God.'
    Upon the awful threshold then he spoke,
    ' How holds in you such insolence abode ?
Why kick against that will which never broke
    Short of its end, if ever it begin,
    And often for you fiercer torments woke ?
Butting 'gainst fate, what can ye hope to win ?
    Your Cerberus, as is to you well known,
    Still bears for this a well-peeled throat and chin.'
Then by the passage foul he back was gone, 100
    Nor spake to us, but like a man was he
    By other cares absorbed and driven on
Than that of those who may around him be.
    And we, confiding in the sacred word,
    Moved toward the town in all security.
We entered without hindrance, and I, spurred
    By my desire the character to know
    And style of place such strong defences gird,

Entering, begin mine eyes around to throw,
    And see on every hand a vast champaign,   110
    The teeming seat of torments and of woe.
And as at Arles where Rhone spreads o'er the plain,
    Or Pola, hard upon Quarnaro sound
    Which bathes the boundaries Italian,
The sepulchres uneven make the ground ;
    So here on every side, but far more dire
    And grievous was the fashion of them found.
For scattered 'mid the tombs blazed many a fire,
    Because of which these with such fervour burned
    No arts which work in iron more require.   120
All of the lids were lifted.   I discerned
    By keen laments which from the tombs arose
    That sad and suffering ones were there inurned.
I said : ' O Master, tell me who are those
    Buried within the tombs, of whom the sighs
    Come to our ears thus eloquent of woes ?'
And he to me : ' The lords of heresies
    With followers of all sects, a greater band
    Than thou wouldst think, these sepulchres comprise.
To lodge them like to like the tombs are planned.   130
    The sepulchres have more or less of heat.'
    Then passed we, turning to the dexter hand,
'Tween torments and the lofty parapet.

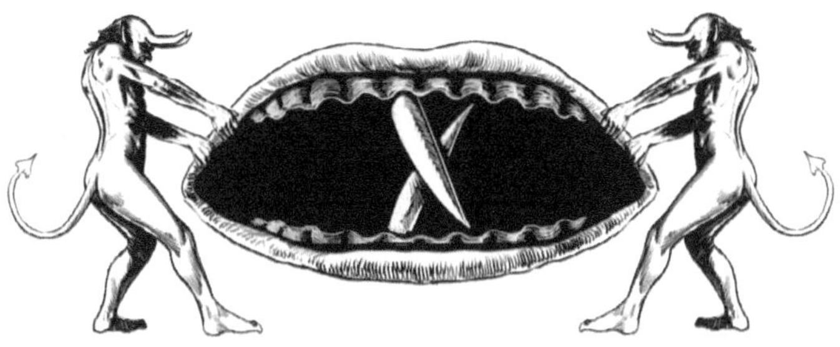

The Sixth Circle continued ✣ Farinata degli Uberti ✣ Cavalcante dei Cavalcanti ✣ Farinata's prophecy ✣ Frederick II

AND NOW ADVANCE we by a narrow track
    Between the torments and the ramparts high,
    My Master first, and I behind his back.
' O mighty Virtue, at whose will am I
    Wheeled through these impious circles,' then I said,
    ' Speak, and in full my longing satisfy.
The people who within the tombs are laid,
    May they be seen ?   The coverings are all thrown
    Open, nor is there any guard displayed.'
And he to me :   ' All shall be fastened down   10
    When hither from Jehoshaphat they come
    Again in bodies which were once their own.
All here with Epicurus find their tomb
    Who are his followers, and by whom 'tis held
    That the soul shares the body's mortal doom.
Things here discovered then shall answer yield,
    And quickly, to thy question asked of me ;
    As well as to the wish thou hast concealed.'
And I :   ' Good Leader, if I hide from thee
    My heart, it is that I may little say ;   20
    Nor only now learned I thus dumb to be.'
' O Tuscan, who, still living, mak'st thy way,
    Modest of speech, through the abode of flame,
    Be pleased a little in this place to stay.
The accents of thy language thee proclaim
    To be a native of that state renowned
    Which I, perchance, wronged somewhat.' Sudden came
These words from out a tomb which there was found
    'Mongst others ; whereon I, compelled by fright,
    A little toward my Leader shifted ground.   30

FARINATA DEGLI UBERTI
Canto X, lines 14 - 54

And he : ' Turn round, what ails thee ?   Lo ! upright
    Beginneth Farinatato arise ;
    All of him 'bove the girdle comes in sight.'
On him already had I fixed mine eyes.
    Towering erect with lifted front and chest,
    He seemed Inferno greatly to despise.
And toward him I among the tombs was pressed
    By my Guide's nimble and courageous hand,
    While he, ' Choose well thy language,' gave behest.
Beneath his tomb when I had ta'en my stand   40
    Regarding me a moment, ' Of what house
    Art thou ?' as if in scorn, he made demand.
To show myself obedient, anxious,
    I nothing hid, but told my ancestors ;
    And, listening, he gently raised his brows.
' Fiercely to me they proved themselves adverse,
    And to my sires and party,' then he said ;
    ' Because of which I did them twice disperse.'
I answered him :   ' And what although they fled !
    Twice from all quarters they returned with might,   50
    An art not mastered yet by these you led.'
Beside him then there issued into sight
    Another shade, uncovered to the chin,
    Propped on his knees, if I surmised aright.
He peered around as if he fain would win
    Knowledge if any other was with me ;
    And then, his hope all spent, did thus begin,
Weeping :   ' By dint of genius if it be
    Thou visit'st this dark prison, where my son ?
    And wherefore not found in thy company ?'   60
And I to him : ' I come not here alone :
    He waiting yonder guides me : but disdain
    Of him perchance was by your Guido shown.'
The words he used, and manner of his pain,
    Revealed his name to me beyond surmise ;
    Hence was I able thus to answer plain.
Then cried he, and at once upright did rise,
    ' How saidst thou—was ?   Breathes he not then the air ?
    The pleasant light no longer smites his eyes ?'

When he of hesitation was aware   70
        Displayed by me in forming my reply,
        He fell supine, no more to reappear.
But the magnanimous, at whose bidding I
        Had halted there, the same expression wore,
        Nor budged a jot, nor turned his neck awry.
' And if'—resumed he where he paused before—
        ' They be indeed but slow that art to learn,
        Than this my bed, to hear it pains me more.
But ere the fiftieth time anew shall burn
        The lady's face who reigneth here below,   80
        Of that sore art thou shalt experience earn.
And as to the sweet world again thou'dst go,
        Tell me, why is that people so without
        Ruth for my race, as all their statutes show ?'
And I to him :   ' The slaughter and the rout
        Which made the Arbiato run with red,
        Cause in our fane such prayers to be poured out.'
Whereon he heaved a sigh and shook his head :
        ' There I was not alone, nor to embrace
        That cause was I, without good reason, led.   90
But there I was alone, when from her place
        All granted Florence should be swept away.
        'Twas I defended her with open face.'
' So may your seed find peace some better day.'
        I urged him, ' as this knot you shall untie
        In which my judgment doth entangled stay.
If I hear rightly, ye, it seems, descry
        Beforehand what time brings, and yet ye seem
        'neath other laws as touching what is nigh.'
' Like those who see best what is far from them,   100
        We see things,' said he, ' which afar remain ;
        Thus much enlightened by the Guide Supreme.
To know them present or approaching, vain
        Are all our powers ; and save what they relate
        Who hither come, of earth no news we gain.
Hence mayst thou gather in how dead a state
        Shall all our knowledge from that time be thrown
        When of the future shall be closed the gate.'

Then, for my fault as if repentant grown,
    I said : ' Report to him who fell supine,   110
    That still among the living breathes his son.
And if I, dumb, seemed answer to decline,
    Tell him it was that I upon the knot
    Was pondering then, you helped me to untwine.'
Me now my Master called, whence I besought
    With more than former sharpness of the shade,
    To tell me what companions he had got.
He answered me : ' Some thousand here are laid
    With me ; 'mong these the Second Frederick,
    The Cardinal too ; of others nought be said.'   120
Then was he hid ; and towards the Bard antique
    I turned my steps, revolving in my brain
    The ominous words which I had heard him speak.
He moved, and as we onward went again
    Demanded of me : ' Wherefore thus amazed ?'
    And to his question I made answer plain.
' Within thy mind let there be surely placed.'
    The Sage bade, ' what 'gainst thee thou heardest say.
    Now mark me well' (his finger here he raised),
' When thou shalt stand within her gentle ray   130
    Whose beauteous eye sees all, she will make known
    The stages of thy journey on life's way.'
Turning his feet, he to the left moved on ;
    Leaving the wall, we to the middle went
    Upon a path that to a vale strikes down,
Which even to us above its foulness sent.

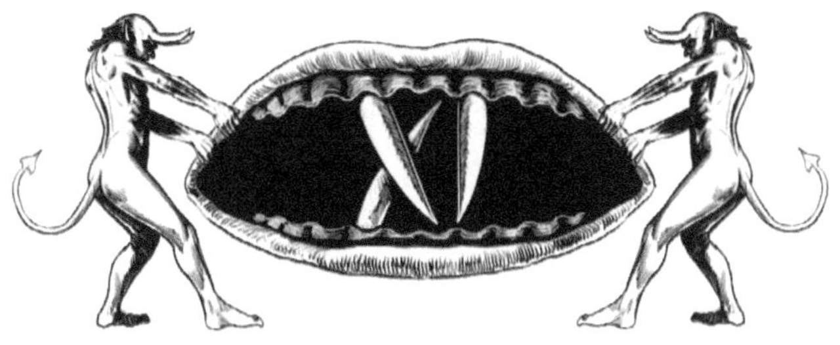

The Sixth Circle continued ❧ Pope Anastasius ❧ Virgil explains
on what principle sinners are classified in Inferno ❧ Usury

WE AT THE MARGIN of a lofty steep
    Made of great shattered stones in circle bent,
    Arrived where worser torments crowd the deep.
So horrible a stench and violent
    Was upward wafted from the vast abyss,
    Behind the cover we for shelter went
Of a great tomb where I saw written this :
    ' Pope Anastasius is within me thrust,
    Whom the straight way Photinus made to miss.'
' Now on our course a while we linger must.'   10
    The Master said, ' be but our sense resigned
    A little to it, and the filthy gust
We shall not heed.'   Then I :   ' Do thou but find
    Some compensation lest our time should run
    Wasted.'   And he :   ' Behold, 'twas in my mind.
Girt by the rocks before us, O my son,
    Lie three small circles,' he began to tell,
    ' Graded like those with which thou now hast done,
All of them filled with spirits miserable.
    That sight of them may thee henceforth suffice.   20
    Hear how and wherefore in these groups they dwell.
Whate'er in Heaven's abhorred as wickedness
    Has injury for its end ; in others' bane
    By fraud resulting or in violent wise.
Since fraud to man alone doth appertain,
    God hates it most ; and hence the fraudulent band,
    Set lowest down, endure a fiercer pain.
Of the violent is the circle next at hand
    To us ; and since three ways is violence shown,
    'tis in three several circuits built and planned.   30

POPE ANASTASIUS
Canto XI, lines 1 - 27

To God, ourselves, or neighbours may be done
    Violence, or on the things by them possessed ;
    As reasoning clear shall unto thee make known.
Our neighbour may by violence be distressed
    With grievous wounds, or slain ; his goods and lands
    By havoc, fire, and plunder be oppressed.
Hence those who wound and slay with violent hands,
    Robbers, and spoilers, in the nearest round
    Are all tormented in their various bands.

Violent against himself may man be found,   40
    And 'gainst his goods ; therefore without avail
    They in the next are in repentance drowned
Who on themselves loss of your world entail,
    Who gamble and their substance madly spend,
    And who when called to joy lament and wail.
And even to God may violence extend
    By heart denial and by blasphemy,
    Scorning what nature doth in bounty lend.
Sodom and Cahors hence are doomed to lie
    Within the narrowest circlet surely sealed ;   50
    And such as God within their hearts defy.
Fraud, 'gainst whose bite no conscience findeth shield,
    A man may use with one who in him lays
    Trust, or with those who no such credence yield.
Beneath this latter kind of it decays
    The bond of love which out of nature grew ;
    Hence, in the second circle herd the race
To feigning given and flattery, who pursue
    Magic, false coining, theft, and simony,
    Pimps, barrators, and suchlike residue.   60
The other form of fraud makes nullity
    Of natural bonds ; and, what is more than those,
    The special trust whence men on men rely.
Hence in the place whereon all things repose,
    The narrowest circle and the seat of Dis,
    Each traitor's gulfed in everlasting woes.'
' Thy explanation, Master, as to this
    Is clear,' I said, ' and thou hast plainly told
    Who are the people stowed in the abyss.
But tell why those the muddy marshes hold,   70
    The tempest-driven, those beaten by the rain,
    And such as, meeting, virulently scold,
Are not within the crimson city ta'en
    For punishment, if hateful unto God ;
    And, if not hateful, wherefore doomed to pain ?'
And he to me :   ' Why wander thus abroad,
    More than is wont, thy wits ? Or how engrossed
    Is now thy mind, and on what things bestowed ?

Hast thou the memory of the passage lost
    In which thy Ethics for their subject treat   80
    Of the three moods by Heaven abhorred the most—
Malice and bestiality complete ;
    And how, compared with these, incontinence
    Offends God less, and lesser blame doth meet ?
If of this doctrine thou extract the sense,
    And call to memory what people are
    Above, outside, in endless penitence,
Why from these guilty they are sundered far
    Thou shalt discern, and why on them alight
    The strokes of justice in less angry war.'   90
' O Sun that clearest every troubled sight,
    So charmed am I by thy resolving speech,
    Doubt yields me joy no less than knowing right.
Therefore, I pray, a little backward reach.'
    I asked, ' to where thou say'st that usury
    Sins 'gainst God's bounty ; and this mystery teach.'
He said :   ' Who gives ear to Philosophy
    Is taught by her, nor in one place alone,
    What nature in her course is governed by,
Even Mind Divine, and art which thence hath grown ;   100
    And if thy Physics thou wilt search within,
    Thou'lt find ere many leaves are open thrown,
This art by yours, far as your art can win,
    Is followed close—the teacher by the taught ;
    As grandchild then to God your art is kin.
And from these two—do thou recall to thought
    How Genesis begins—should come supplies
    Of food for man, and other wealth be sought.
And, since another plan the usurer plies,
    Nature and nature's child have his disdain ;   110
    Because on other ground his hope relies.
But come, for to advance I now am fain :
    The Fishes over the horizon line
    Quiver ; o'er Caurus now stands all the Wain ;
And further yonder does the cliff decline.'

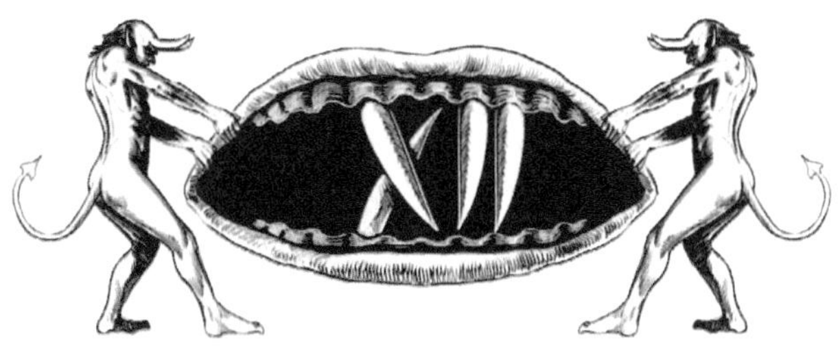

THE PLACE of our descent before us lay
     Precipitous, and there was something more
     From sight of which all eyes had turned away.
As at the ruin which upon the shore
     Of Adige fell upon this side of Trent—
     Through earthquake or by slip of what before
Upheld it—from the summit whence it went
     Far as the plain, the shattered rocks supply
     Some sort of foothold to who makes descent ;
Such was the passage down the precipice high.   10
     And on the riven gully's very brow
     Lay spread at large the Cretan Infamy
Which was conceived in the pretended cow.
     Us when he saw, he bit himself for rage
     Like one whose anger gnaws him through and through.
' Perhaps thou deemest,' called to him the Sage,
     ' This is the Duke of Athens drawing nigh,
     Who war to the death with thee on earth did wage.
Begone, thou brute, for this one passing by
     Untutored by thy sister has thee found,   20
     And only comes thy sufferings to spy.'
And as the bull which snaps what held it bound
     On being smitten by the fatal blow,
     Halts in its course, and reels upon the ground,
The Minotaur I saw reel to and fro ;
     And he, the alert, cried :   ' To the passage haste ;
     While yet he chafes 'twere well thou down shouldst go.'
So we descended by the slippery waste
     Of shivered stones which many a time gave way
     'neath the new weight my feet upon them placed.   30

THE MINOTAUR
Canto XII, lines 12 - 36

I musing went ; and he began to say :
     ' Perchance this ruined slope thou thinkest on,
     Watched by the brute rage I did now allay.
But I would have thee know, when I came down
     The former time into this lower Hell,
     The cliff had not this ruin undergone.
It was not long, if I distinguish well,
     Ere He appeared who wrenched great prey from Dis
     From out the up most circle.   Trembling fell
Through all its parts the nauseous abyss   40
     With such a violence, the world, I thought,
     Was stirred by love ; for, as they say, by this
She back to Chaos has been often brought.
     And then it was this ancient rampart strong
     Was shattered here and at another spot.
But toward the valley look.   We come ere long
     Down to the river of blood where boiling lie
     All who by violence work others wrong.'
O insane rage ! O blind cupidity !
     By which in our brief life we are so spurred,   50
     Ere downward plunged in evil case for aye !
An ample ditch I now beheld engird
     And sweep in circle all around the plain,
     As from my Escort I had lately heard.
Between this and the rock in single train
     Centaurs were running who were armed with bows,
     As if they hunted on the earth again.
Observing us descend they all stood close,
     Save three of them who parted from the band
     With bow, and arrows they in coming chose.   60
' What torment,' from afar one made demand,
     ' Come ye to share, who now descend the hill ?
     I shoot unless ye answer whence ye stand.'
My Master said :   ' We yield no answer till
     We come to Chiron standing at thy side ;
     But thy quick temper always served thee ill.'
Then touching me :   ' 'Tis Nessus ; he who died
     With love for beauteous Dejanire possessed,
     And who himself his own vendetta plied.

THE CENTAURS
Canto XII, lines 58 - 84

He in the middle, staring on his breast,   70
    Is mighty Chiron, who Achilles bred ;
    And next the wrathful Pholus.   They invest
The fosse and in their thousands round it tread,
    Shooting whoever from the blood shall lift,
    More than his crime allows, his guilty head.'
As we moved nearer to those creatures swift
    Chiron drew forth a shaft and dressed his beard
    Back on his jaws, using the arrow's cleft.
And when his ample mouth of hair was cleared,
    He said to his companions : ' Have ye seen   80
    The things the second touches straight are stirred,
As they by feet of shades could ne'er have been ?'
    And my good Guide, who to his breast had gone—
    The part where join the natures, ' Well I ween
He lives,' made answer ; ' and if, thus alone,
    He seeks the valley dim 'neath my control,
    Necessity, not pleasure, leads him on.
One came from where the alleluiahs roll,
    Who charged me with this office strange and new :
    No robber he, nor mine a felon soul.   90
But, by that Power which makes me to pursue
    The rugged journey whereupon I fare,
    Accord us one of thine to keep in view,
That he may show where lies the ford, and bear
    This other on his back to yonder strand ;
    No spirit he, that he should cleave the air.'
Wheeled to the right then Chiron gave command
    To Nessus : ' Turn, and lead them, and take tent
    They be not touched by any other band.'
We with our trusty Escort forward went,   100
    Threading the margin of the boiling blood
    Where they who seethed were raising loud lament.
People I saw up to the chin imbrued,
    ' These all are tyrants,' the great Centaur said,
    ' Who blood and plunder for their trade pursued.
Here for their pitiless deeds tears now are shed
    By Alexander, and Dionysius fell,
    Through whom in Sicily dolorous years were led.

THE TYRANTS
Canto XII, lines 85 - 110

The forehead with black hair so terrible
    Is Ezzelino ; that one blond of hue,   110
    Obizzo d'Este, whom, as rumours tell,
His stepson murdered, and report speaks true.'
    I to the Poet turned, who gave command :
    ' Regard thou chiefly him.   I follow you.'
Ere long the Centaur halted on the strand,
    Close to a people who, far as the throat,
    Forth of that bulicamë seemed to stand.
Thence a lone shade to us he pointed out
    Saying :   ' In God's house ran he weapon through
    The heart which still on Thames wins cult devout.'   120
Then I saw people, some with heads in view,
    And some their chests above the river bore ;
    And many of them I, beholding, knew.
And thus the blood went dwindling more and more,
    Until at last it covered but the feet :
    Here took we passage to the other shore.
' As on this hand thou seest still abate
    In depth the volume of the boiling stream.'
    The Centaur said, ' so grows its depth more great,
Believe me, towards the opposite extreme,   130
    Until again its circling course attains
    The place where tyrants must lament.   Supreme
Justice upon that side involves in pains,
    With Attila, once of the world the pest,
    Pyrrhus and Sextus : and for ever drains
Tears out of Rinier of Corneto pressed
    And Rinier Pazzo in that boiling mass,
    Whose brigandage did so the roads infest.'
Then turned he back alone, the ford to pass.

THE HARPIES
Canto XIII, lines 1 - 12

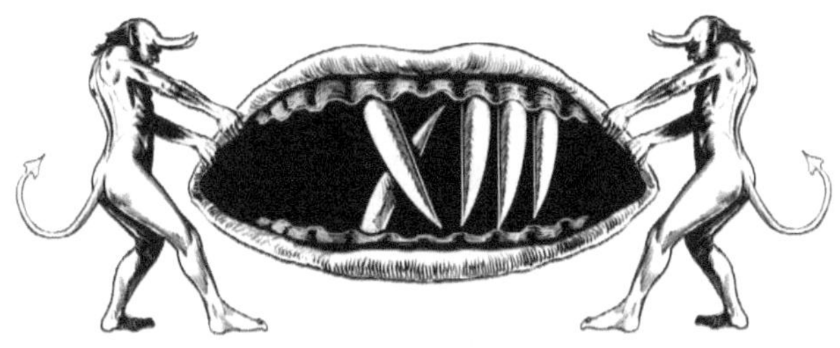

*The Seventh Circle continued the Second Division consisting of a Tangled Wood
in which are those guilty of Violence against themselves the Harpies Pier
delle Vigne Lano Jacopo da Sant' Andrea Florence and its Patrons*

ERE NESSUS LANDED on the other shore
    We for our part within a forest drew,
    Which of no pathway any traces bore.
Not green the foliage, but of dusky hue ;
    Not smooth the boughs, but gnarled and twisted round ;
    For apples, poisonous thorns upon them grew.
No rougher brakes or matted worse are found
    Where savage beasts betwixt Corneto roam
    And Cecina, abhorring cultured ground.
The loathsome Harpies nestle here at home,   10
    Who from the Strophades the Trojans chased
    With dire predictions of a woe to come.
Great winged are they, but human necked and faced,
    With feathered belly, and with claw for toe ;
    They shriek upon the bushes wild and waste.
' Ere passing further, I would have thee know.'
    The worthy Master thus began to say,
    ' Thou'rt in the second round, nor hence shalt go
Till by the horrid sand thy footsteps stay.
    Give then good heed, and things thou'lt recognise   20
    That of my words will prove the verity.'
Wailings on every side I heard arise :
    Of who might raise them I distinguished nought ;
    Whereon I halted, smitten with surprise.
I think he thought that haply 'twas my thought
    The voices came from people 'mong the trees,
    Who, to escape us, hiding-places sought ;
Wherefore the Master said : ' From one of these
    Snap thou a twig, and thou shalt understand
    How little with thy thought the fact agrees.'   30

Thereon a little I stretched forth my hand
  And plucked a tiny branch from a great thorn.
  'Why dost thou tear me ?' made the trunk demand.
When dark with blood it had begun to turn,
  It cried a second time : 'Why wound me thus ?
  Doth not a spark of pity in thee burn ?
Though trees we be, once men were all of us ;
  Yet had our souls the souls of serpents been
  Thy hand might well have proved more piteous.'
As when the fire hath seized a fagot green   40
  At one extremity, the other sighs,
  And wind, escaping, hisses ; so was seen,
At where the branch was broken, blood to rise
  And words were mixed with it. I dropped the spray
  And stood like one whom terror doth surprise.
The Sage replied : ' Soul vexed with injury,
  Had he been only able to give trust
  To what he read narrated in my lay,
His hand toward thee would never have been thrust.
  'Tis hard for faith ; and I, to make it plain,   50
  Urged him to trial, mourn it though I must.
But tell him who thou wast ; so shall remain
  This for amends to thee, thy fame shall blow
  A fresh on earth, where he returns again.'
And then the trunk : ' Thy sweet words charm me so,
  I cannot dumb remain ; nor count it hard
  If I some pains upon my speech bestow.
For I am he who held both keys in ward
  Of Frederick's heart, and turned them how I would,
  And softly oped it, and as softly barred,   60
Till scarce another in his counsel stood.
  To my high office I such loyalty bore,
  It cost me sleep and haleness of my blood.
The harlot who removeth nevermore
  From Cæsar's house eyes ignorant of shame—
  A common curse, of courts the special sore—
Set against me the minds of all aflame,
  And these in turn Augustus set on fire,
  Till my glad honours bitter woes became.

My soul, filled full with a disdainful ire,   70
    Thinking by means of death disdain to flee,
    'Gainst my just self unjustly did conspire.
I swear even by the new roots of this tree
    My fealty to my lord I never broke,
    For worthy of all honour sure was he.
If one of you return 'mong living folk,
    Let him restore my memory, overthrown
    And suffering yet because of envy's stroke.'
Still for a while the poet listened on,
    Then said : ' Now he is dumb, lose not the hour,   80
    But make request if more thou'dst have made known.'
And I replied : ' Do thou inquire once more
    Of what thou thinkest I would gladly know ;
    I cannot ask ; ruth wrings me to the core.'
On this he spake :   ' Even as the man shall do,
    And liberally, what thou of him hast prayed,
    Imprisoned spirit, do thou further show
How with these knots the spirits have been made
    Incorporate ; and, if thou canst, declare
    If from such members e'er is loosed a shade.'   90
Then from the trunk came vehement puffs of air ;
    Next, to these words converted was the wind :
    ' My answer to you shall be short and clear.
When the fierce soul no longer is confined
    In flesh, torn thence by action of its own,
    To the Seventh Depth by Minos 'tis consigned.
No choice is made of where it shall be thrown
    Within the wood ; but where by chance 'tis flung
    It germinates like seed of spelt that's sown.
A forest tree it grows from sapling young ;   100
    Eating its leaves, the Harpies cause it pain,
    And open loopholes whence its sighs are wrung.
We for our vestments shall return again
    Like others, but in them shall ne'er be clad :
    Men justly lose what from themselves they've ta'en.
Dragged hither by us, all throughout the sad
    Forest our bodies shall be hung on high ;
    Each on the thorn of its destructive shade.'

RAVENOUS AND FLEET
Canto XIII, lines 124 - 129

While to the trunk we listening lingered nigh,
　　Thinking he might proceed to tell us more,　　　　110
　　A sudden uproar we were startled by
Like him who, that the huntsman and the boar
　　To where he stands are sweeping in the chase,
　　Knows by the crashing trees and brutish roar.
Upon our left we saw a couple race
　　Naked and scratched ; and they so quickly fled
　　The forest barriers burst before their face.

‘ Speed to my rescue, death !’ the foremost pled.
    The next, as wishing he could use more haste ;
    ‘ Not thus, O Lano, thee thy legs bested   120
When one at Toppo’s tournament thou wast.’
    Then, haply wanting breath, aside he stepped,
    Merged with a bush on which himself he cast.
Behind them through the forest onward swept
    A pack of dogs, black, ravenous, and fleet,
    Like greyhounds from their leashes newly slipped.
In him who crouched they made their teeth to meet,
    And, having piecemeal all his members rent,
    Haled them away enduring anguish great.
Grasping my hand, my Escort forward went   130
    And led me to the bush which, all in vain,
    Through its ensanguined openings made lament.
‘ James of St. Andrews,’ it we heard complain ;
    ‘ What profit hadst thou making me thy shield ?
    For thy bad life doth blame to me pertain ?’
Then, halting there, this speech my Master held :
    ‘ Who wast thou that through many wounds dost sigh,
    Mingled with blood, words big with sorrow swelled ?’
‘ O souls that hither come,’ was his reply,
    ‘ To witness shameful outrage by me borne,   140
    Whence all my leaves torn off around me lie,
Gather them to the root of this drear thorn.
    My city for the Baptist changed of yore
    Her former patron ; wherefore, in return,
He with his art will make her aye deplore ;
    And were it not some image doth remain
    Of him where Arno’s crossed from shore to shore,
Those citizens who founded her again
    On ashes left by Attila, had spent
    Their labour of a surety all in vain.   150
In my own house I up a gibbet went.’

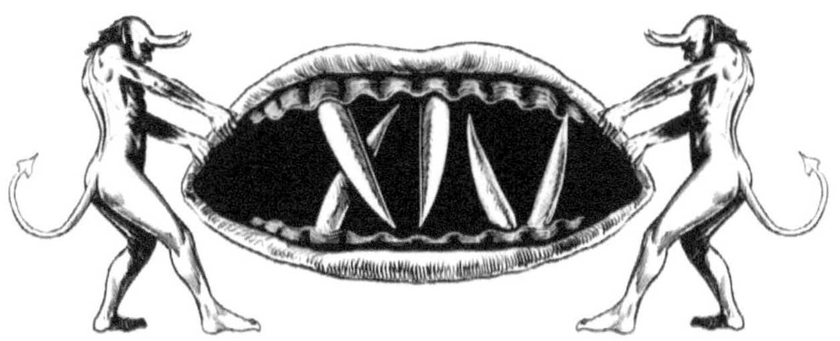

ME OF MY NATIVE PLACE the dear constraint
 Led to restore the leaves which round were strewn,
 To him whose voice by this time was grown faint.
Thence came we where the second round joins on
 Unto the third, wherein how terrible
 The art of justice can be, is well shown.
But, clearly of these wondrous things to tell,
 I say we entered on a plain of sand
 Which from its bed doth every plant repel.
The dolorous wood lies round it like a band,   10
 As that by the drear fosse is circled round.
 Upon its very edge we came to a stand.
And there was nothing within all that bound
 But burnt and heavy sand ; like that once trod
 Beneath the feet of Cato was the ground.
Ah, what a terror, O revenge of God !
 Shouldst thou awake in any that may read
 Of what before mine eyes was spread abroad.
I of great herds of naked souls took heed.
 Most piteously was weeping every one ;   20
 And different fortunes seemed to them decreed.
For some of them upon the ground lay prone,
 And some were sitting huddled up and bent,
 While others, restless, wandered up and down.
More numerous were they that roaming went
 Than they that were tormented lying low ;
 But these had tongues more loosened to lament.
O'er all the sand, deliberate and slow,
 Broad open flakes of fire were downward rained,
 As 'mong the Alps in calm descends the snow.   30

SHOWER OF FIRE
Canto XIV, lines 12 - 36

Such Alexander saw when he attained
  The hottest India ; on his host they fell
  And all unbroken on the earth remained ;
Wherefore he bade his phalanxes tread well
  The ground, because when taken one by one
  The burning flakes they could the better quell.
So here eternal fire was pouring down ;
  As tinder 'neath the steel, so here the sands
  Kindled, whence pain more vehement was known.
And, dancing up and down, the wretched hands 40
  Beat here and there for ever without rest ;
  Brushing away from them the falling brands.
And I : ' O Master, by all things confessed
  Victor, except by obdurate evil powers
  Who at the gate to stop our passage pressed,
Who is the enormous one who noway cowers
  Beneath the fire ; with fierce disdainful air
  Lying as if untortured by the showers ?'
And that same shade, because he was aware
  That touching him I of my Guide was fain 50
  To learn, cried : ' As in life, myself I bear
In death. Though Jupiter should tire again
  His smith, from whom he snatched in angry bout
  The bolt by which I at the last was slain ;
Though one by one he tire the others out
  At the black forge in Mongibello placed,
  While " Ho, good Vulcan, help me !" he shall shout—
The cry he once at Phlegra's battle raised ;
  Though hurled with all his might at me shall fly
  His bolts, yet sweet revenge he shall not taste.' 60
Then spake my Guide, and in a voice so high
  Never till then heard I from him such tone :
  ' O Capaneus, because unquenchably
Thy pride doth burn, worse pain by thee is known.
  Into no torture save thy madness wild
  Fit for thy fury couldest thou be thrown.'
Then, to me turning with a face more mild,
  He said : ' Of the Seven Kings was he of old,
  Who leaguered Thebes, and as he God reviled

THE INFERNO

THE STATUE OF TIME
Canto XIV, lines 88 - 115

Him in small reverence still he seems to hold ;   70
  But for his bosom his own insolence
  Supplies fit ornament,as now I told.
Now follow ; but take heed lest passing hence
  Thy feet upon the burning sand should tread ;
  But keep them firm where runs the forest fence.'
We reached a place—nor any word we said—
  Where issues from the wood a streamlet small ;
  I shake but to recall its colour red.
Like that which does from Bulicamë fall,
  And lose ! women later 'mong them share ; 80
  So through the sand this brooklet's waters crawl.
Its bottom and its banks I was aware
  Were stone, and stone the rims on either side.
  From this I knew the passage must be there.
' Of all that I have shown thee as thy guide
  Since when we by the gateway entered in,
  Whose threshold unto no one is denied,
Nothing by thee has yet encountered been
  So worthy as this brook to cause surprise,
  O'er which the falling fire-flakes quenched are seen.' 90
These were my Leader's words. For full supplies
  I prayed him of the food of which to taste
  Keen appetite he made within me rise.
' In middle sea there lies a country waste,
  Known by the name of Crete,' I then was told,
  ' Under whose king the world of yore was chaste.
There stands a mountain, once the joyous hold
  Of woods and streams ; as Ida 'twas renowned,
  Now 'tis deserted like a thing grown old.
For a safe cradle 'twas by Rhea found.   100
  To nurse her child in ; and his infant cry,
  Lest it betrayed him, she with clamours drowned.
Within the mount an old man towereth high.
  Towards Damietta are his shoulders thrown ;
  On Rome, as on his mirror, rests his eye.
His head is fashioned of pure gold alone ;
  Of purest silver are his arms and chest ;
  'Tis brass to where his legs divide ; then down

From that is all of iron of the best,
    Save the right foot, which is of baken clay ;
    And upon this foot doth he chiefly rest.
Save what is gold, doth every part display
    A fissure dripping tears ; these, gathering all
    Together, through the grotto pierce a way.
From rock to rock into this deep they fall,
    Feed Acheron and Styx and Phlegethon,
    Then downward travelling by this strait canal,
Far as the place where further slope is none,
    Cocytus form ; and what that pool may be
    I say not now.   Thou'lt see it further on.'
' If this brook rises,' he was asked by me,
    ' Within our world, how comes it that no trace
    We saw of it till on this boundary ?'
And he replied :   ' Thou knowest that the place
    Is round, and far as thou hast moved thy feet,
    Still to the left hand sinking to the base,
Nath'less thy circuit is not yet complete.
    Therefore if something new we chance to spy,
    Amazement needs not on thy face have seat.'
I then :   ' But, Master, where doth Lethe lie,
    And Phlegethon ?   Of that thou sayest nought ;
    Of this thou say'st, those tears its flood supply.'
' It likes me well to be by thee besought ;
    But by the boiling red wave,' I was told,
    ' To half thy question was an answer brought.
Lethe, not in this pit, shalt thou behold.
    Thither to wash themselves the spirits go,
    When penitence has made them spotless souled.'
Then said he :   ' From the wood 'tis fitting now
    That we depart ; behind me press thou nigh.
    Keep we the margins, for they do not glow,
And over them, ere fallen, the fire-flakes die.'

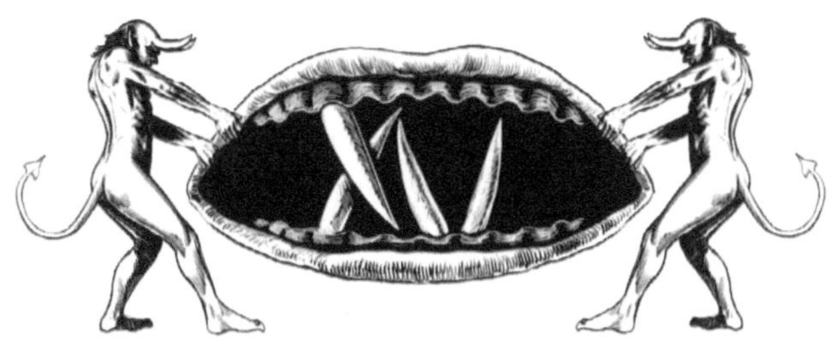

The Seventh Circle continued   *the Violent against Nature*   *Brunetto Latini*
  Francesco d'Accorso   *Andrea de' Mozzi, Bishop of Florence*

NOW LIES OUR WAY along one of the margins hard ;
    Steam rising from the rivulet forms a cloud,
    Which 'gainst the fire doth brook and borders guard.
Like walls the Flemings, timorous of the flood
    Which towards them pours betwixt Bruges and Cadsand,
    Have made, that ocean's charge may be withstood ;
Or what the Paduans on the Brenta's strand
    To guard their castles and their homesteads rear,
    Ere Chiarentana feel the spring-tide bland ;
Of the same fashion did those dikes appear,   10
    Though not so high he made them, nor so vast,
    Whoe'er the builder was that piled them here.
We, from the wood when we so far had passed
    I should not have distinguished where it lay
    Though I to see it backward glance had cast,
A group of souls encountered on the way,
    Whose line of march was to the margin nigh.
    Each looked at us—as by the new moon's ray
Men peer at others 'neath the darkening sky—
    Sharpening his brows on us and only us,   20
    Like an old tailor on his needle's eye.
And while that crowd was staring at me thus,
    One of them knew me, caught me by the gown,
    And cried aloud :   ' Lo, this is marvellous !'
And straightway, while he thus to me held on,
    I fixed mine eyes upon his fire-baked face,
    And, spite of scorching, seemed his features known,
And whose they were my memory well could trace ;
    And I, with hand stretched toward his face below,
    Asked :   ' Ser Brunetto ! and is this your place ?'   30

BRUNETTO LATINI
Canto XV, lines 13 - 124

' O son,' he answered, ' no displeasure show,
    If now Brunetto Latini shall some way
    Step back with thee, and leave his troop to go.'
I said :   ' With all my heart for this I pray,
    And, if you choose, I by your side will sit ;
    If he, for I go with him, grant delay.'
' Son,' said he, ' who of us shall intermit
    Motion a moment, for an age must lie
    Nor fan himself when flames are round him lit.
On, therefore !   At thy skirts I follow nigh,   40
    Then shall I overtake my band again,
    Who mourn a loss large as eternity.'
I dared not from the path step to the plain
    To walk with him, but low I bent my head,
    Like one whose steps are all with reverence ta'en.
' What fortune or what destiny,' he said,
    ' Hath brought thee here or e'er thou death hast seen ;
    And who is this by whom thou'rt onward led ?'
' Up yonder,' said I, ' in the life serene,
    I in a valley wandered all forlorn   50
    Before my years had full accomplished been.
I turned my back on it but yestermorn ;
    Again I sought it when he came in sight
    Guided by whom I homeward thus return.'
And he to me :   ' Following thy planet's light
    Thou of a glorious haven canst not fail,
    If in the blithesome life I marked aright.
And had my years known more abundant tale,
    Seeing the heavens so held thee in their grace
    I, heartening thee, had helped thee to prevail.   60
But that ungrateful and malignant race
    Which down from Fiesole came long ago,
    And still its rocky origin betrays,
Will for thy worthiness become thy foe ;
    And with good reason, for 'mong crab-trees wild
    It ill befits the mellow fig to grow.
By widespread ancient rumour are they styled
    A people blind, rapacious, envious, vain :
    See by their manners thou be not defiled.

Fortune reserves such honour for thee, fain   70
    Both sides will be to enlist thee in their need ;
    But from the beak the herb shall far remain.
Let beasts of Fiesole go on to tread
    Themselves to litter, nor the plants molest,
    If any such now spring on their rank bed,
In whom there flourishes indeed the blest
    Seed of the Romans who still lingered there
    When of such wickedness 'twas made the nest.'
' Had I obtained full answer to my prayer,
    You had not yet been doomed,' I then did say,   80
    ' This exile from humanity to bear.
For deep within my heart and memory
    Lives the paternal image good and dear
    Of you, as in the world, from day to day,
How men escape oblivion you made clear ;
    My thankfulness for which shall in my speech
    While I have life, as it behoves, appear.
I note what of my future course you teach.
    Stored with another text it will be glozed
    By one expert, should I that Lady reach.   90
Yet would I have this much to you disclosed :
    If but my conscience no reproaches yield,
    To all my fortune is my soul composed.
Not new to me the hint by you revealed ;
    Therefore let Fortune turn her wheel apace,
    Even as she will ; the clown his mattock wield.'
Thereon my Master right about did face,
    And uttered this, with glance upon me thrown :
    ' He hears to purpose who doth mark the place.'
And none the less I, speaking, still go on   100
    With Ser Brunetto ; asking him to tell
    Who of his band are greatest and best known.
And he to me :   ' To hear of some is well,
    But of the rest 'tis fitting to be dumb,
    And time is lacking all their names to spell.
That all of them were clerks, know thou in sum,
    All men of letters, famous and of might ;
    Stained with one sin all from the world are come.

Priscian goes with that crowd of evil plight,
    Francis d'Accorso too ; and hadst thou mind   110
    For suchlike trash thou mightest have had sight
Of him the Slave of Slaves to change assigned
    From Arno's banks to Bacchiglione, where
    His nerves fatigued with vice he left behind.
More would I say, but neither must I fare
    Nor talk at further length, for from the sand
    I see new dust-clouds rising in the air,
I may not keep with such as are at hand.
    Care for my *Treasure* ; for I still survive
    In that my work.　I nothing else demand.'   120
Then turned he back, and ran like those who strive
    For the Green Cloth upon Verona's plain ;
    And seemed like him that shall the first arrive,
And not like him that labours all in vain.

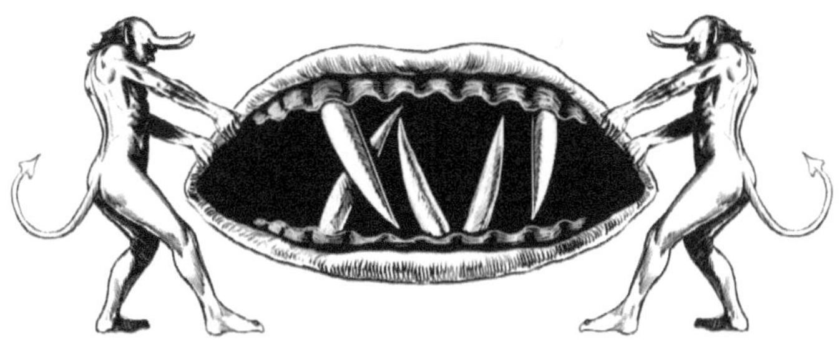

NOW COULD I HEAR the water as it fell
    To the next circle with a murmuring sound
    Like what is heard from swarming hives to swell ;
When three shades all together with a bound
    Burst from a troop met by us pressing on
    'neath rain of that sharp torment.   O'er the ground
Toward us approaching, they exclaimed each one :
    ' Halt thou, whom from thy garb we judge to be
    A citizen of our corrupted town.'
Alas, what scars I on their limbs did see,   10
    Both old and recent, which the flames had made :
    Even now my ruth is fed by memory.
My Teacher halted at their cry, and said :
    ' Await a while :' and looked me in the face ;
    ' Some courtesy to these were well displayed.
And but that fire—the manner of the place—
    Descends for ever, fitting 'twere to find
    Rather than them, thee quickening thy pace.'
When we had halted, they again combined
    In their old song ; and, reaching where we stood,   20
    Into a wheel all three were intertwined.
And as the athletes used, well oiled and nude,
    To feel their grip and, wary, watch their chance,
    Ere they to purpose strike and wrestle could ;
So each of them kept fixed on me his glance
    As he wheeled round,and in opposing ways
    His neck and feet seemed ever to advance.
' Ah, if the misery of this sand-strewn place
    Bring us and our petitions in despite.'
    One then began, ' and flayed and grimy face ;   30

THREE GENTLEMEN OF FLORENCE
Canto XVI, lines 22 - 42

Let at the least our fame goodwill incite
    To tell us who thou art, whose living feet
    Thus through Inferno wander without fright.
For he whose footprints, as thou see'st, I beat,
    Though now he goes with body peeled and nude,
    More than thou thinkest, in the world was great.
The grandson was he of Gualdrada good ;
    He, Guidoguerra, with his armèd hand
    Did mighty things, and by his counsel shrewd.
The other who behind me treads the sand   40
    Is one whose name should on the earth be dear ;
    For he is Tegghiaio Aldobrand.
And I, who am tormented with them here,
    James Rusticucci was ; my fierce and proud
    Wife of my ruin was chief minister.'
If from the fire there had been any shroud
    I should have leaped down 'mong them, nor have earned
    Blame, for my Teacher sure had this allowed.
But since I should have been all baked and burned,
    Terror prevailed the goodwill to restrain   50
    With which to clasp them in my arms I yearned.
Then I began : ' ' Twas not contempt but pain
    Which your condition in my breast awoke,
    Where deeply rooted it will long remain,
When this my Master words unto me spoke,
    By which expectancy was in me stirred
    That ye who came were honourable folk.
I of your city am, and with my word
    Your deeds and honoured names oft to recall
    Delighted, and with joy of them I heard.   60
To the sweet fruits I go, and leave the gall,
    As promised to me by my Escort true ;
    But first I to the centre down must fall.'
' So may thy soul thy members long endue
    With vital power,' the other made reply,
    ' And after thee thy fame its light renew ;
As thou shalt tell if worth and courtesy
    Within our city as of yore remain,
    Or from it have been wholly forced to fly.

For William Borsier, one of yonder train,   70
      And but of late joined with us in this woe,
      Causeth us with his words exceeding pain.'
' Upstarts, and fortunes suddenly that grow,
      Have bred in thee pride and extravagance,
      Whence tears, O Florence ! thou art shedding now.'
Thus cried I with uplifted countenance.
      The three, accepting it for a reply,
      Glanced each at each as hearing truth men glance.
And all :   ' If others thou shalt satisfy
      As well at other times at no more cost,   80
      Happy thus at thine ease the truth to cry !
Therefore if thou escap'st these regions lost,
      Returning to behold the starlight fair,
      Then when " There was I," thou shalt make thy boast,
Something of us do thou 'mong men declare.'
      Then broken was the wheel, and as they fled
      Their nimble legs like pinions beat the air.
So much as one *Amen !* had scarce been said
      Quicker than what they vanished from our view.
      On this once more the way my Master led.   90
I followed, and ere long so near we drew
      To where the water fell, that for its roar
      Speech scarcely had been heard between us two.
And as the stream which of all those which pour
      East (from Mount Viso counting) by its own
      Course falls the first from Apennine to shore—
As Acquacheta in the uplands known
      By name, ere plunging to its bed profound ;
      Name lost ere by Forlì its waters run—
Above St. Benedict with one long bound,   100
      Where for a thousand would be ample room,
      Falls from the mountain to the lower ground ;
Down the steep cliff that water dyed in gloom
      We found to fall echoing from side to side,
      Stunning the ear with its tremendous boom.
There was a cord about my middle tied,
      With which I once had thought that I might hold
      Secure the leopard with the painted hide.

When this from round me I had quite unrolled
  To him I handed it, all coiled and tight ;   110
  As by my Leader I had first been told.
Himself then bending somewhat toward the right,
  He just beyond the edge of the abyss
  Threw down the cord, which disappeared from sight.
' That some strange thing will follow upon this
  Unwonted signal which my Master's eye
  Thus follows,' so I thought, ' can hardly miss.'
Ah, what great caution need we standing by
  Those who behold not only what is done,
  But who have wit our hidden thoughts to spy ! 120
He said to me : ' There shall emerge, and soon,
  What I await ; and quickly to thy view
  That which thou dream'st of shall be clearly known.'
From utterance of truth which seems untrue
  A man, whene'er he can, should guard his tongue ;
  Lest he win blame to no transgression due.
Yet now I must speak out, and by the song
  Of this my Comedy, Reader, I swear—
  So in good liking may it last full long !—
I saw a shape swim upward through that air. 130
  All indistinct with gross obscurity,
  Enough to fill the stoutest heart with fear :
Like one who rises having dived to free
  An anchor grappled on a jagged stone,
  Or something else deep hidden in the sea ;
With feet drawn in and arms all open thrown.

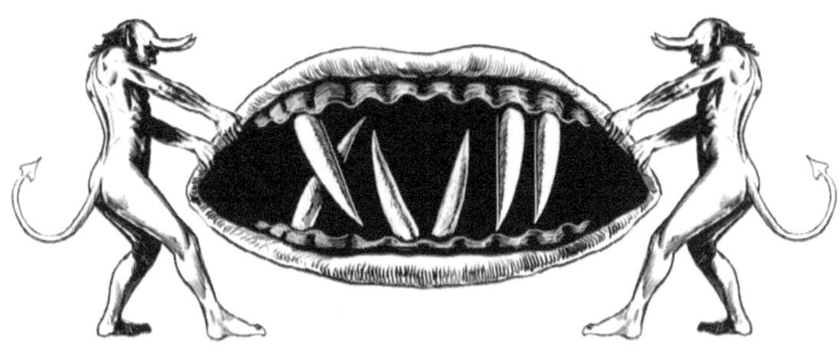

' BEHOLD THE MONSTER with the pointed tail,
    Who passes mountains and can entrance make
    Through arms and walls ! who makes the whole world ail,
Corrupted by him !' Thus my Leader spake,
    And beckoned him that he should land hard by,
    Where short the pathways built of marble break.
And that foul image of dishonesty
    Moving approached us with his head and chest,
    But to the bank drew not his tail on high.
His face a human righteousness expressed,   10
    'twas so benignant to the outward view ;
    A serpent was he as to all the rest.
On both his arms hair to the arm-pits grew :
    On back and chest and either flank were knot
    And rounded shield portrayed in various hue ;
No Turk or Tartar weaver ever brought
    To ground or pattern a more varied dye ;
    Nor by Arachne was such broidery wrought.
As sometimes by the shore the barges lie
    Partly in water, partly on dry land ;   20
    And as afar in gluttonous Germany,
Watching their prey, alert the beavers stand ;
    So did this worst of brutes his foreparts fling
    Upon the stony rim which hems the sand.
All of his tail in space was quivering,
    Its poisoned fork erecting in the air,
    Which scorpion-like was armèd with a sting.
My Leader said : ' Now we aside must fare
    A little distance, so shall we attain
    Unto the beast malignant crouching there.'   30

THE GERYON
Canto XVII, lines 1 - 31

So we stepped down upon the right, and then
 A half score steps to the outer edge did pace,
 Thus clearing well the sand and fiery rain.
And when we were hard by him I could trace
 Upon the sand a little further on
 Some people sitting near to the abyss.
' That what this belt containeth may be known
 Completely by thee,' then the Master said ;
 ' To see their case do thou advance alone.
Let thy inquiries be succinctly made.   40
 While thou art absent I will ask of him,
 With his strong shoulders to afford us aid.'
Then, all alone, I on the outmost rim
 Of that Seventh Circle still advancing trod,
 Where sat a woful folk. Full to the brim
Their eyes with anguish were, and overflowed ;
 Their hands moved here and there to win some ease,
 Now from the flames, now from the soil which glowed.
No otherwise in summer-time one sees,
 Working its muzzle and its paws, the hound 50
 When bit by gnats or plagued with flies or fleas.
And I, on scanning some who sat around
 Of those on whom the dolorous flames alight,
 Could recognise not one. I only found
A purse hung from the throat of every wight,
 Each with its emblem and its special hue ;
 And every eye seemed feasting on the sight.
As I, beholding them, among them drew,
 I saw what seemed a lion's face and mien
 Upon a yellow purse designed in blue. 60
Still moving on mine eyes athwart the scene
 I saw another scrip, blood-red, display
 A goose more white than butter could have been.
And one, on whose white wallet blazoned lay
 A pregnant sow in azure, to me said :
 ' What dost thou in this pit ? Do thou straightway
Begone ; and, seeing thou art not yet dead,
 Know that Vitalian, neighbour once of mine,
 Shall on my left flank one day find his bed.

A Paduan I : all these are Florentine ;   70
    And oft they stun me, bellowing in my ear :
    " Come, Pink of Chivalry, for whom we pine,
Whose is the purse on which three beaks appear : '"
    Then he from mouth awry his tongue thrust out
    Like ox that licks its nose ; and I, in fear
Lest more delay should stir in him some doubt
    Who gave command I should not linger long,
    Me from those wearied spirits turned about.
I found my Guide, who had already sprung
    Upon the back of that fierce animal :   80
    He said to me :   ' Now be thou brave and strong.
By stairs like this we henceforth down must fall.
    Mount thou in front, for I between would sit
    So thee the tail shall harm not nor appal.'
Like one so close upon the shivering fit
    Of quartan ague that his nails grow blue,
    And seeing shade he trembles every whit,
I at the hearing of that order grew ;
    But his threats shamed me, as before the face
    Of a brave lord his man grows valorous too.   90
On the great shoulders then I took my place,
    And wished to say, but could not move my tongue
    As I expected :   ' Do thou me embrace !'
But he, who other times had helped me 'mong
    My other perils, when ascent I made
    Sustained me, and strong arms around me flung,
And, ' Geryon, set thee now in motion !' said ;
    ' Wheel widely ; let thy downward flight be slow ;
    Think of the novel burden on thee laid.'
As from the shore a boat begins to go   100
    Backward at first, so now he backward pressed,
    And when he found that all was clear below,
He turned his tail where earlier was his breast ;
    And, stretching it, he moved it like an eel,
    While with his paws he drew air toward his chest.
More terror Phaëthon could hardly feel
    What time he let the reins abandoned fall,
    Whence Heaven was fired, as still its tracts reveal ;

Nor wretched Icarus, on finding all
    His plumage moulting as the wax grew hot,   110
    While, ' The wrong road !' his father loud did call ;
Than what I felt on finding I was brought
    Where nothing was but air and emptiness ;
    For save the brute I could distinguish nought.
He slowly, slowly swims ; to the abyss
    Wheeling he makes descent, as I surmise
    From wind felt 'neath my feet and in my face.
Already on the right I heard arise
    From out the caldron a terrific roar,
    Whereon I stretch my head with down-turned eyes.   120
Terror of falling now oppressed me sore ;
    Hearing laments, and seeing fires that burned,
    My thighs I tightened, trembling more and more.
Earlier I had not by the eye discerned
    That we swept downward ; scenes of torment now
    Seemed drawing nearer wheresoe'er we turned.
And as a falcon (which long time doth go
    Upon the wing, not finding lure or prey),
    While ' Ha !' the falconer cries, ' descending so !'
Comes wearied back whence swift it soared away ;   130
    Wheeling a hundred times upon the road,
    Then, from its master far, sulks angrily :
So we, by Geryon in the deep bestowed,
    Were 'neath the sheer-hewn precipice set down :
    He, suddenly delivered from our load,
Like arrow from the string was swiftly gone.

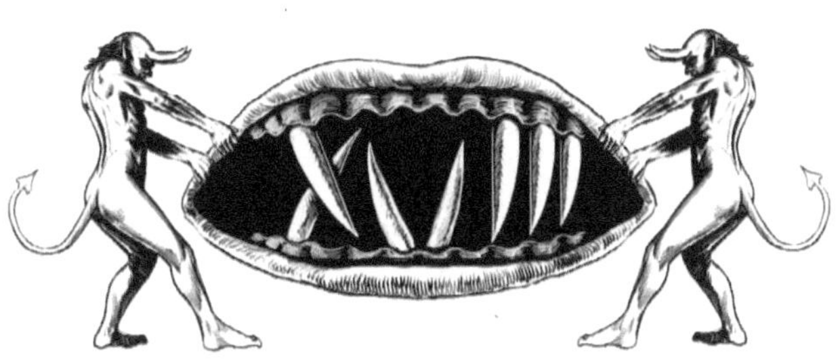

The Eighth Circle, named Malebolge consists of ten concentric Pits or Moats connected by bridges of rock
☙ in these are punished those guilty of Fraud of different kinds ☙ First Bolgia or Moat, where are
Panders and Seducers, scourged by Demons ☙ Venedico Caccianimico ☙ Jason ☙
Second Bolgia, where are Flatterers plunged in filth ☙ Alessio Interminei

OF IRON COLOUR, and composed of stone,
 A place called Malebolge is in Hell,
 Girt by a cliff of substance like its own.
In that malignant region yawns a well
 Right in the centre, ample and profound;
 Of which I duly will the structure tell.
The zone that lies between them, then, is round—
 Between the well and precipice hard and high;
 Into ten vales divided is the ground.
As is the figure offered to the eye,   10
 Where numerous moats a castle's towers enclose
 That they the walls may better fortify;
A like appearance was made here by those.
 And as, again, from threshold of such place
 Many a drawbridge to the outworks goes;
So ridges from the precipice's base
 Cutting athwart the moats and barriers run,
 Till at the well join the extremities.
From Geryon's back when we were shaken down
 'Twas here we stood, until the Poet's feet   20
 Moved to the left, and I, behind, came on.
New torments on the right mine eyes did meet
 With new tormentors, novel woe on woe;
 With which the nearer Bolgia was replete.
Sinners, all naked, in the gulf below,
 This side the middle met us ; while they strode
 On that side with us, but more swift did go.
Even so the Romans, that the mighty crowd
 Across the bridge, the year of Jubilee,
 Might pass with ease, ordained a rule of road—   30

THE SEDUCERS
Canto XVIII, lines 13 - 45

Facing the Castle, on that side should be
    The multitude which to St. Peter's hied ;
    So to the Mount on this was passage free.
On the grim rocky ground, on either side,
    I saw horned devils armed with heavy whip
    Which on the sinners from behind they plied.
Ah, how they made the wretches nimbly skip
    At the first lashes ; no one ever yet
    But sought from the second and the third to slip.
And as I onward went, mine eyes were set   40
    On one of them ; whereon I called in haste :
    ' This one already I have surely met !'
Therefore to know him, fixedly I gazed ;
    And my kind Leader willingly delayed,
    While for a little I my course retraced.
On this the scourged one, thinking to evade
    My search, his visage bent without avail,
    For :   ' Thou that gazest on the ground,' I said,
' If these thy features tell trustworthy tale,
    Venedico Caccianimico thou !   50
    But what has brought thee to such sharp regale ?'
And he, ' I tell it 'gainst my will, I trow,
    But thy clear accents to the old world bear
    My memory, and make me all avow.
I was the man who Ghisola the fair
    To serve the Marquis' evil will led on,
    Whatever the uncomely tale declare.
Of Bolognese here weeping not alone
    Am I ; so full the place of them, to-day
    'Tween Reno and Savenaare not known   60
So many tongues that *Sipa* deftly say :
    And if of this thou'dst know the reason why,
    Think but how greedy were our hearts alway.'
To him thus speaking did a demon cry :
    ' Pander, begone !' And smote him with his thong ;
    ' Here are no women for thy coin to buy.'
Then, with my Escort joined, I moved along.
    Few steps we made until we there had come,
    Where from the bank a rib of rock was flung.

THE FLATTERERS
Canto XVIII, lines 91 - 117

With ease enough up to its top we clomb,   70
    And, turning on the ridge, bore to the right ;
    And those eternal circles parted from.
When we had reached where underneath the height
    A passage opes, yielding the scourged a way,
    My Guide bade : ' Tarry, so to hold in sight
Those other spirits born in evil day,
    Whose faces until now from thee have been
    Concealed, because with ours their progress lay.'
Then from the ancient bridge by us were seen
    The troop which toward us on that circuit sped,   80
    Chased onward, likewise, by the scourges keen.
And my good Master, ere I asked him, said :
    ' That lordly one now coming hither, see,
    By whom, despite of pain, no tears are shed.
What mien he still retains of majesty !
    'Tis Jason, who by courage and by guile
    The Colchians of the ram deprived.   ' Twas he
Who on his passage by the Lemnian isle,
    Where all of womankind with daring hand
    Upon their males had wrought a murder vile,   90
With loving pledges and with speeches bland
    The tender-yeared Hypsipyle betrayed,
    Who had herself a fraud on others planned.
Forlorn he left her then, when pregnant made.
    That is the crime condemns him to this pain ;
    And for Medea too is vengeance paid.
Who in his manner cheat compose his train.
    Of the first moat sufficient now is known,
    And those who in its jaws engulfed remain.'
Already had we by the strait path gone   100
    To where 'tis with the second bank dovetailed—
    The buttress whence a second arch is thrown.
Here heard we who in the next Bolgia wailed
    And puffed for breath ; reverberations told
    They with their open palms themselves assailed.
The sides were crusted over with a mould
    Plastered upon them by foul mists that rise,
    And both with eyes and nose a contest hold.

The bottom is so deep, in vain our eyes
    Searched it till further up the bridge we went,   110
    To where the arch o'erhangs what under lies.
Ascended there, our eyes we downward bent,
    And I saw people in such ordure drowned,
    A very cesspool 'twas of excrement.
And while I from above am searching round,
    One with a head so filth-smeared I picked out,
    I knew not if 'twas lay, or tonsure-crowned.
'Why then so eager,' asked he with a shout,
    'To stare at me of all the filthy crew?'
    And I to him: 'Because I scarce can doubt   120
That formerly thee dry of hair I knew,
    Alessio Interminei the Lucchese;
    And therefore thee I chiefly hold in view.'
Smiting his head-piece, then, his words were these:
    ''Twas flattery steeped me here; for, using such,
    My tongue itself enough could never please.'
'Now stretch thou somewhat forward, but not much.'
    Thereon my Leader bade me, 'and thine eyes
    Slowly advance till they her features touch
And the dishevelled baggage recognise,   130
    Clawing her yonder with her nails unclean,
    Now standing up, now squatting on her thighs.
'tis harlot Thais, who, when she had been
    Asked by her lover, "Am I generous
    And worthy thanks?" Said, "Greatly so, I ween."
Enough of this place has been seen by us.'

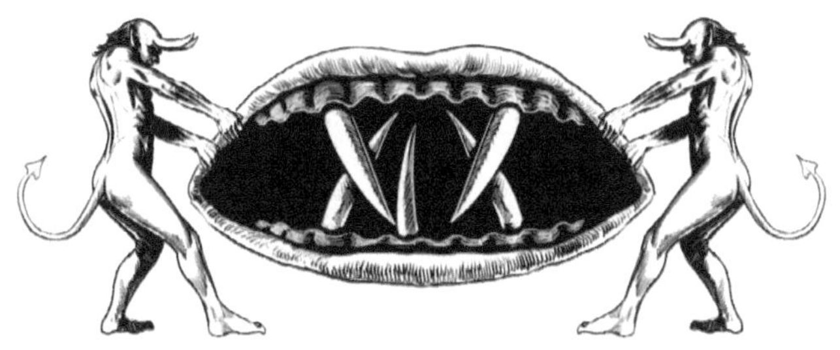

The Eighth Circle ❧ Third Bolgia, where are the Simoniacs, stuck head downwards in holes in the rock ❧ Pope Nicholas III. ❧ the Donation of Constantine

O SIMON MAGUS ! ye his wretched crew !
    The gifts of God, ordained to be the bride
    Of righteousness, ye prostitute that you
With gold and silver may be satisfied ;
    Therefore for you let now the trumpet blow,
    Seeing that ye in the Third Bolgia 'bide.
Arrived at the next tomb, we to the brow
    Of rock ere this had finished our ascent,
    Which hangs true plumb above the pit below.
What perfect art, O Thou Omniscient,   10
    Is Thine in Heaven and earth and the bad world found !
    How justly does Thy power its dooms invent !
The livid stone, on both banks and the ground,
    I saw was full of holes on every side,
    All of one size, and each of them was round.
No larger seemed they to me nor less wide
    Than those within my beautiful St. John
    For the baptizers' standing-place supplied ;
And one of which, not many years agone,
    I broke to save one drowning ; and I would   20
    Have this for seal to undeceive men known.
Out of the mouth of each were seen protrude
    A sinner's feet, and of the legs the small
    Far as the calves ; the rest enveloped stood.
And set on fire were both the soles of all,
    Which made their ankles wriggle with such throes
    As had made ropes and withes asunder fall.
And as flame fed by unctuous matter goes
    Over the outer surface only spread ;
    So from their heels it flickered to the toes.   30

THE SIMONIACS
Canto XIX, lines 1 - 15

' Master, who is he, tortured more,' I said,
     ' Than are his neighbours, writhing in such woe ;
     And licked by flames of deeper-hearted red ?'
And he :   ' If thou desirest that below
     I bear thee by that bank which lowest lies,
     Thou from himself his sins and name shalt know.'
And I :   ' Thy wishes still for me suffice :
     Thou art my Lord, and knowest I obey
     Thy will ; and dost my hidden thoughts surprise.'
To the fourth barrier then we made our way,   40
     And, to the left hand turning, downward went
     Into the narrow hole-pierced cavity ;
Nor the good Master caused me make descent
     From off his haunch till we his hole were nigh
     Who with his shanks was making such lament.
' Whoe'er thou art, soul full of misery,
     Set like a stake with lower end upcast.'
     I said to him, ' Make, if thou canst, reply.'
I like a friar stood who gives the last
     Shrift to a vile assassin, to his side   50
     Called back to win delay for him fixed fast.
' Art thou arrived already ?' Then he cried,
     ' Art thou arrived already, Boniface ?
     By several years the prophecy has lied.
Art so soon wearied of the wealthy place,
     For which thou didst not fear to take with guile,
     Then ruin the fair Lady ?'   Now my case
Was like to theirs who linger on, the while
     They cannot comprehend what they are told,
     And as befooled from further speech resile.   60
But Virgil bade me :   ' Speak out loud and bold,
     " I am not he thou thinkest, no, not he ! "'
     And I made answer as by him controlled.
The spirit's feet then twisted violently,
     And, sighing in a voice of deep distress,
     He asked :   ' What then requirest thou of me ?
If me to know thou hast such eagerness,
     That thou the cliff hast therefore ventured down,
     Know, the Great Mantle sometime was my dress.

I of the Bear, in sooth, was worthy son :   70
      As once, the Cubs to help, my purse with gain
      I stuffed, myself I in this purse have stown.
Stretched out at length beneath my head remain
      All the simoniacs that before me went,
      And flattened lie throughout the rocky vein.
I in my turn shall also make descent,
      Soon as he comes who I believed thou wast,
      When I asked quickly what for him was meant.
O'er me with blazing feet more time has past,
      While upside down I fill the topmost room,   80
      Than he his crimsoned feet shall upward cast ;
For after him one viler still shall come,
      A Pastor from the West, lawless of deed :
      To cover both of us his worthy doom.
A modern Jason he, of whom we read
      In Maccabees, whose King denied him nought :
      With the French King so shall this man succeed.'
Perchance I ventured further than I ought,
      But I spake to him in this measure free :
      ' Ah, tell me now what money was there sought   90
Of Peter by our Lord, when either key
      He gave him in his guardianship to hold ?
      Sure He demanded nought save :   " Follow me ! "
Nor Peter, nor the others, asked for gold
      Or silver when upon Matthias fell
      The lot instead of him, the traitor-souled.
Keep then thy place, for thou art punished well,
      And clutch the pelf, dishonourably gained,
      Which against Charles made thee so proudly swell.
And, were it not that I am still restrained   100
      By reverence for those tremendous keys,
      Borne by thee while the glad world thee contained,
I would use words even heavier than these ;
      Seeing your avarice makes the world deplore,
      Crushing the good, filling the bad with ease.
'twas you, O Pastors, the Evangelist bore
      In mind what time he saw her on the flood
      Of waters set, who played with kings the whore ;

Who with seven heads was born ; and as she would
    By the ten horns to her was service done,   110
    Long as her spouse rejoiced in what was good
Now gold and silver are your god alone :
    What difference 'twixt the idolater and you,
    Save that ye pray a hundred for his one ?
Ah, Constantine, how many evils grew—
    Not from thy change of faith, but from the gift
    Wherewith thou didst the first rich Pope endue !'
While I my voice continued to uplift
    To such a tune, by rage or conscience stirred
    Both of his soles he made to twist and shift.   120
My Guide, I well believe, with pleasure heard ;
    Listening he stood with lips so well content
    To me propounding truthful word on word.
Then round my body both his arms he bent,
    And, having raised me well upon his breast,
    Climbed up the path by which he made descent.
Nor was he by his burden so oppressed
    But that he bore me to the bridge's crown,
    Which with the fourth joins the fifth rampart's crest.
And lightly here he set his burden down,   130
    Found light by him upon the precipice,
    Up which a goat uneasily had gone.
And thence another valley met mine eyes.

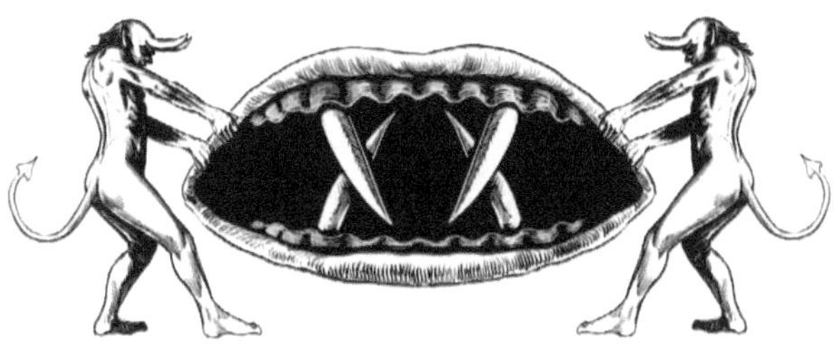

*The Eighth Circle ❧ Fourth Bolgia, where are Diviners and Sorcerers in endless procession,
with their heads twisted on their necks ❧ Amphiaräus, Tiresias, Aruns, Manto and
the foundation of Mantua: Eurypylus, Michael Scott, Guido Bonatti, and Asdente*

NOW OF NEW TORMENT must my verses tell,
    And matter for the Twentieth Canto win
    Of Lay the First, which treats of souls in Hell.
Already was I eager to begin
    To peer into the visible profound,
    Which tears of agony was bathèd in :
And I saw people in the valley round ;
    Like that of penitents on earth the pace
    At which they weeping came, nor uttering sound.
When I beheld them with more downcast gaze,   10
    That each was strangely screwed about I learned,
    Where chest is joined to chin.   And thus the face
Of every one round to his loins was turned ;
    And stepping backward all were forced to go,
    For nought in front could be by them discerned.
Smitten by palsy although one might show
    Perhaps a shape thus twisted all awry,
    I never saw, and am to think it slow.
As, Reader, God may grant thou profit by
    Thy reading, for thyself consider well   20
    If I could then preserve my visage dry
When close at hand to me was visible
    Our human form so wrenched that tears, rained down
    Out of the eyes, between the buttocks fell.
In very sooth I wept, leaning upon
    A boss of the hard cliff, till on this wise
    My Escort asked :   ' Of the other fools art one ?
Here piety revives as pity dies ;
    For who more irreligious is than he
    In whom God's judgments to regret give rise ?   30

DIVINERS AND SORCERERS
Canto XX, lines 1 - 12

Lift up, lift up thy head, and thou shalt see
    Him for whom earth yawned as the Thebans saw,
    All shouting meanwhile :   " Whither dost thou flee,
Amphiaraüs ?   Wherefore thus withdraw
    From battle ?" But he sinking found no rest
    Till Minos clutched him with all-grasping claw.
Lo, how his shoulders serve him for a breast !
    Because he wished to see too far before
    Backward he looks, to backward course addressed.
Behold Tiresias, who was changed all o'er,   40
    Till for a man a woman met the sight,
    And not a limb its former semblance bore ;
And he behoved a second time to smite
    The same two twisted serpents with his wand,
    Ere he again in manly plumes was dight.
With back to him, see Aruns next at hand,
    Who up among the hills of Luni, where
    Peasants of near Carrara till the land,
Among the dazzling marbles held his lair
    Within a cavern, whence could be descried   50
    The sea and stars of all obstruction bare.
The other one, whose flowing tresses hide
    Her bosom, of the which thou seest nought,
    And all whose hair falls on the further side,
Was Manto ; who through many regions sought :
    Where I was born, at last her foot she stayed.
    It likes me well thou shouldst of this be taught.
When from this life her father exit made,
    And Bacchus' city had become enthralled,
    She for long time through many countries strayed.   60
'Neath mountains by which Germany is walled
    And bounded at Tirol, a lake there lies
    High in fair Italy, Benacus called.
The waters of a thousand springs that rise
    'Twixt Val Camonica and Garda flow
    Down Pennine ; and their flood this lake supplies.
And from a spot midway, if they should go
    Thither, the Pastors of Verona, Trent,
    And Brescia might their blessings all bestow.

Peschiera, with its strength for ornament,   70
          Facing the Brescians and the Bergamese
          Lies where the bank to lower curve is bent.
And there the waters, seeking more of ease,
          For in Benacus is not room for all,
          Forming a river, lapse by green degrees.
The river, from its very source, men call
          No more Benacus—'tis as Mincio known,
          Which into Po does at Governo fall.
A flat it reaches ere it far has run,
          Spreading o'er which it feeds a marshy fen,   80
          Whence oft in summer pestilence has grown.
Wayfaring here the cruel virgin, when
          She found land girdled by the marshy flood,
          Untilled and uninhabited of men,
That she might 'scape all human neighbourhood
          Stayed on it with her slaves, her arts to ply ;
          And there her empty body was bestowed.
On this the people from the country nigh
          Into that place came crowding, for the spot,
          Girt by the swamp, could all attack defy,   90
And for the town built o'er her body sought
          A name from her who made it first her seat,
          Calling it Mantua, without casting lot.
The dwellers in it were in number great,
          Till stupid Casalodi was befooled
          And victimised by Pinamonte's cheat.
Hence, shouldst thou ever hear (now be thou schooled !)
          Another story to my town assigned,
          Let by no fraud the truth be overruled.'
And I :   'Thy reasonings, Master, to my mind   100
          So cogent are, and win my faith so well,
          What others say I shall black embers find.
But of this people passing onward tell,
          If thou, of any, something canst declare,
          For all my thoughts on that intently dwell.'
And then he said :   'The one whose bearded hair
          Falls from his cheeks upon his shoulders dun,
          Was, when the land of Greece of males so bare

Was grown the very cradles scarce held one,
  An augur ; he with Calchas gave the sign   110
  In Aulis through the first rope knife to run.
Eurypylus was he called, and in some line
  Of my high Tragedy is sung the same,
  As thou know'st well, who mad'st it wholly thine.
That other, thin of flank, was known to fame
  As Michael Scott ; and of a verity
  He knew right well the black art's inmost game.
Guido Bonatti, and Asdente see
  Who mourns he ever should have parted from
  His thread and leather ; but too late mourns he. 120
Lo the unhappy women who left loom,
  Spindle, and needle that they might divine ;
  With herb and image hastening men's doom.
But come ; for where the hemispheres confine
  Cain and the Thorns is falling, to alight
  Underneath Seville on the ocean line.
The moon was full already yesternight ;
  Which to recall thou shouldst be well content,
  For in the wood she somewhat helped thy plight.'
Thus spake he to me while we forward went. 130

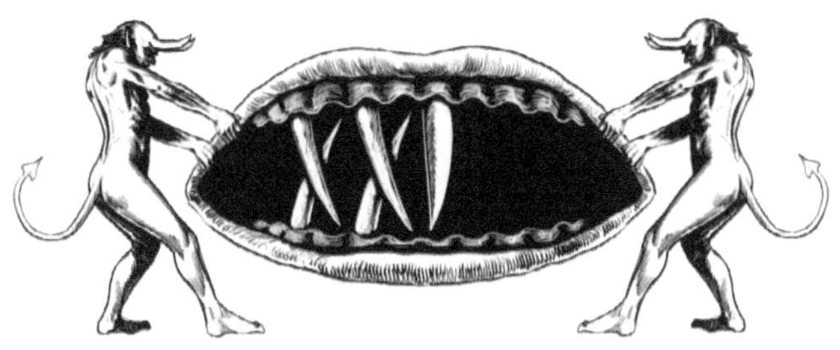

The Eighth Circle   Fifth Bolgia, where the Barrators, or corrupt officials, are plunged in the boiling pitch which fills the Bolgia   a Senator of Lucca is thrown in   the Malebranche, or Demons who guard the Moat   the Devilish Escort

CONVERSING STILL from bridge to bridge we went ;
    But what our words I in my Comedy
    Care not to tell.   The top of the ascent
Holding, we halted the next pit to spy
    Of Malebolge, with plaints bootless all :
    There, darkness full of wonder met the eye.
As the Venetians in their Arsenal
    Boil the tenacious pitch at winter-tide,
    To caulk the ships with for repairs that call ;
For then they cannot sail ; and so, instead,   10
    One builds his bark afresh, one stops with tow
    His vessel's ribs, by many a voyage tried ;
One hammers at the poop, one at the prow ;
    Some fashion oars, and others cables twine,
    And others at the jib and main sails sew :
So, not by fire, but by an art Divine,
    Pitch of thick substance boiled in that low Hell,
    And all the banks did as with plaster line.
I saw it, but distinguished nothing well
    Except the bubbles by the boiling raised,   20
    Now swelling up and ceasing now to swell.
While down upon it fixedly I gazed,
    ' Beware, beware !' my Leader to me said,
    And drew me thence close to him.   I, amazed,
Turned sharply round, like him who has delayed,
    Fain to behold the thing he ought to flee,
    Then, losing nerve, grows suddenly afraid,
Nor lingers longer what there is to see ;
    For a black devil I beheld advance
    Over the cliff behind us rapidly.   30

THE ELDER OF LUCCA
Canto XXI, lines 13 - 49

Ah me, how fierce was he of countenance !
    What bitterness he in his gesture put,
    As with spread wings he o'er the ground did dance !
Upon his shoulders, prominent and acute,
    Was perched a sinner fast by either hip ;
    And him he held by tendon of the foot.
He from our bridge :   'Ho, Malebranche ! Grip
    An Elder brought from Santa Zita's town :
    Stuff him below ; myself once more I slip
Back to the place where lack of such is none.   40
    There, save Bonturo, barrates every man,
    And No grows Yes that money may be won.'
He shot him down, and o'er the cliff began
    To run ; nor unchained mastiff o'er the ground,
    Chasing a robber, swifter ever ran.
The other sank, then rose with back bent round ;
    But from beneath the bridge the devils cried :
    ' Not here the Sacred Countenance is found,
One swims not here as on the Serchio's tide ;
    So if thou wouldst not with our grapplers deal   50
    Do not on surface of the pitch abide.'
Then he a hundred hooks was made to feel.
    ' Best dance down there,' they said the while to him,
    ' Where, if thou canst, thou on the sly mayst steal.'
So scullions by the cooks are set to trim
    The caldrons and with forks the pieces steep
    Down in the water, that they may not swim.
And the good Master said to me :   ' Now creep
    Behind a rocky splinter for a screen ;
    So from their knowledge thou thyself shalt keep.   60
And fear not thou although with outrage keen
    I be opposed, for I am well prepared,
    And formerly have in like contest been.'
Then passing from the bridge's crown he fared
    To the sixth bank, and when thereon he stood
    He needed courage doing what he dared.
In the same furious and tempestuous mood
    In which the dogs upon the beggar leap,
    Who, halting suddenly, seeks alms or food,

THE MALEBRANCHE
Canto XXI, lines 115 - 133

They issued forth from underneath the deep   70
      Vault of the bridge, with grapplers 'gainst him stretched ;
      But he exclaimed :   ' Aloof, and harmless keep !
Ere I by any of your hooks be touched,
      Come one of you and to my words give ear ;
      And then advise you if I should be clutched.'
All cried :   ' Let Malacoda then go near ;'
      On which one moved, the others standing still.
      He coming said :   ' What will this help him here ?'
' O Malacoda, is it credible
      That I am come,' my Master then replied,   80
      ' Secure your opposition to repel,
Without Heaven's will, and fate, upon my side ?
      Let me advance, for 'tis by Heaven's behest
      That I on this rough road another guide.'
Then was his haughty spirit so depressed,
      He let his hook drop sudden to his feet,
      And, ' Strike him not !' commanded all the rest
My Leader charged me thus :   ' Thou, from thy seat
      Where 'mid the bridge's ribs thou crouchest low,
      Rejoin me now in confidence complete.'   90
Whereon I to rejoin him was not slow ;
      And then the devils, crowding, came so near,
      I feared they to their paction false might show.
So at Caprona saw I footmen fear,
      Spite of their treaty, when a multitude
      Of foes received them, crowding front and rear.
With all my body braced I closer stood
      To him, my Leader, and intently eyed
      The aspect of them, which was far from good.
Lowering their grapplers, 'mong themselves they cried :   100
      ' Shall I now tickle him upon the thigh ?'
      ' Yea, see thou clip him deftly,' one replied.
The demon who in parley had drawn nigh
      Unto my Leader, upon this turned round ;
      ' Scarmiglione, lay thy weapon by !'
He said ; and then to us :   ' No way is found
      Further along this cliff, because, undone,
      All the sixth arch lies ruined on the ground.

But if it please you further to pass on,
    Over this rocky ridge advancing climb   110
    To the next rib, where passage may be won.
Yestreen, but five hours later than this time,
    Twelve hundred sixty-six years reached an end,
    Since the way lost the wholeness of its prime.
Thither I some of mine will straightway send
    To see that none peer forth to breathe the air :
    Go on with them ; you they will not offend.
You, Alichin and Calcabrin, prepare
    To move,' he bade ;   ' Cagnazzo, thou as well ;
    Guiding the ten, thou, Barbariccia, fare.   120
With Draghignazzo, Libicocco fell,
    Fanged Ciriatto, Graffiacane too,
    Set on, mad Rubicant and Farfarel :
Search on all quarters round the boiling glue.
    Let these go safe, till at the bridge they be,
    Which doth unbroken o'er the caverns go.'
' Alas, my Master, what is this I see ?'
    Said I, ' Unguided, let us forward set,
    If thou know'st how.   I wish no company.
If former caution thou dost not forget,   130
    Dost thou not mark how each his teeth doth grind,
    The while toward us their brows are full of threat ?'
And he :   ' I would not fear should fill thy mind ;
    Let them grin all they will, and all they can ;
    'Tis at the wretches in the pitch confined.'
They wheeled and down the left hand bank began
    To march, but first each bit his tongue, and passed
    The signal on to him who led the van.
He answered grossly as with trumpet blast.

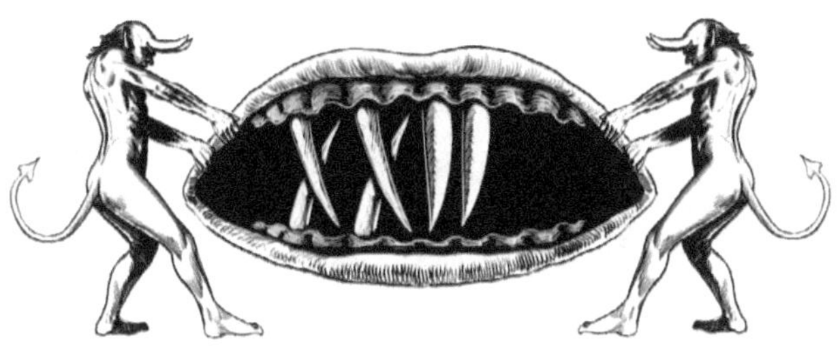

The Eighth Circle ❧ Fifth Bolgia continued ❧ the Navarese ❧ trick played by him on the Demons ❧ Fra Gomita ❧ Michael Zanche ❧ the Demons fall foul of one another

HORSEMEN I'VE SEEN in march across the field,
 Hastening to charge, or, answering muster, stand,
 And sometimes too when forced their ground to yield ;
I have seen skirmishers upon your land,
 O Aretines ! and those on foray sent ;
 With trumpet and with bell to sound command
Have seen jousts run and well-fought tournament,
 With drum, and signal from the castle shown,
 And foreign music with familiar blent ;
But ne'er by blast on such a trumpet blown   10
 Beheld I horse or foot to motion brought,
 Nor ship by star or landmark guided on.
With the ten demons moved we from the spot ;
 Ah, cruel company ! but ' with the good
 In church, and in the tavern with the sot.'
Still to the pitch was my attention glued
 Fully to see what in the Bolgia lay,
 And who were in its burning mass imbrued.
As when the dolphins vaulted backs display,
 Warning to mariners they should prepare   20
 To trim their vessel ere the storm makes way ;
So, to assuage the pain he had to bear,
 Some wretch would show his back above the tide,
 Then swifter plunge than lightnings cleave the air.
And as the frogs close to the marsh's side
 With muzzles thrust out of the water stand,
 While feet and bodies carefully they hide ;
So stood the sinners upon every hand.
 But on beholding Barbariccia nigh
 Beneath the bubbles disappeared the band.   30

I saw what still my heart is shaken by :
    One waiting, as it sometimes comes to pass
    That one frog plunges, one at rest doth lie ;
And Graffiacan, who nearest to him was,
    Him upward drew, clutching his pitchy hair :
    To me he bore the look an otter has.
I of their names ere this was well aware,
    For I gave heed unto the names of all
    When they at first were chosen.   ' Now prepare,

And, Rubicante, with thy talons fall   40
    Upon him and flay well,' with many cries
    And one consent the accursed ones did call.
I said :   ' O Master, if in any wise
    Thou canst, find out who is the wretched wight
    Thus at the mercy of his enemies.'
Whereon my Guide drew full within his sight,
    Asking him whence he came, and he replied :
    ' In kingdom of Navarre I first saw light.
Me servant to a lord my mother tied ;
    Through her I from a scoundrel sire did spring,   50
    Waster of goods and of himself beside.
As servant next to Thiebault, righteous king,
    I set myself to ply barratorship ;
    And in this heat discharge my reckoning.'
And Ciriatto, close upon whose lip
    On either side a boar-like tusk did stand,
    Made him to feel how one of them could rip.
The mouse had stumbled on the wild cat band ;
    But Barbariccia locked him in embrace,
    And, ' Off while I shall hug him !' gave command.   60
Round to my Master then he turned his face :
    ' Ask more of him if more thou wouldest know,
    While he against their fury yet finds grace.'
My Leader asked : ' Declare now if below
    The pitch 'mong all the guilty there lies here
    A Latian ?'   He replied :   ' Short while ago
From one I parted who to them lived near ;
    And would that I might use him still for shield,
    Then hook or claw I should no longer fear.'
Said Libicocco :   ' Too much grace we yield.'   70
    And in the sinner's arm he fixed his hook,
    And from it clean a fleshy fragment peeled.
But seeing Draghignazzo also took
    Aim at his legs, the leader of the Ten
    Turned swiftly round on them with angry look.
On this they were a little quieted ; then
    Of him who still gazed on his wound my Guide
    Without delay demanded thus again :

' Who was it whom, in coming to the side,
  Thou say'st thou didst do ill to leave behind ?'   80
  ' Gomita of Gallura.' he replied,
' A vessel full of fraud of every kind,
  Who, holding in his power his master's foes,
  So used them him they bear in thankful mind ;
For, taking bribes, he let slip all of those,
  He says ; and he in other posts did worse,
  And as a chieftain 'mong barrators rose.
Don Michael Zanche doth with him converse,
  From Logodoro, and with endless din
  They gossip of Sardinian characters.   90
But look, ah me ! how yonder one doth grin.
  More would I say, but that I am afraid
  He is about to claw me on the skin.'
To Farfarel the captain turned his head,
  For, as about to swoop, he rolled his eye,
  And, ' Cursed hawk, preserve thy distance !' said.
' If ye would talk with, or would closer spy.'
  The frighted wretch began once more to say,
  ' Tuscans or Lombards, I will bring them nigh.
But let the Malebranche first give way,   100
  That of their vengeance they may not have fear,
  And I to this same place where now I stay
For me, who am but one, will bring seven near
  When I shall whistle as we use to do
  Whenever on the surface we appear.'
On this Cagnazzo up his muzzle threw,
  Shaking his head and saying : ' Hear the cheat
  He has contrived, to throw himself below.'
Then he who in devices was complete :
  ' Far too malicious, in good sooth,' replied,   110
  ' When for my friends I plan a sorer fate.'
This, Alichin withstood not but denied
  The others' counsel, saying : ' If thou fling
  Thyself hence, thee I strive not to outstride.
But o'er the pitch I'll dart upon the wing.
  Leave we the ridge, and be the bank a shield ;
  And see if thou canst all of us outspring.'

O Reader, hear a novel trick revealed.
    All to the other side turned round their eyes,
    He first who slowest was the boon to yield.   120
In choice of time the Navarrese was wise ;
    Taking firm stand, himself he forward flung,
    Eluding thus their hostile purposes.
Then with compunction each of them was stung,
    But he the most whose slackness made them fail ;
    Therefore he started, ' Caught !' upon his tongue.
But little it bested, nor could prevail
    His wings 'gainst fear.   Below the other went,
    While he with upturned breast aloft did sail.
And as the falcon, when, on its descent,   130
    The wild duck suddenly dives out of sight,
    Returns outwitted back, and malcontent ;
To be befooled filled Calcabrin with spite.
    Hovering he followed, wishing in his mind
    The wretch escaping should leave cause for fight.
When the barrator vanished, from behind
    He on his comrade with his talons fell
    And clawed him, 'bove the moat with him entwined.
The other was a spar-hawk terrible
    To claw in turn ; together then the two   140
    Plunged in the boiling pool.   The heat full well
How to unlock their fierce embraces knew ;
    But yet they had no power to rise again,
    So were their wings all plastered o'er with glue.
Then Barbariccia, mourning with his train,
    Caused four to fly forth to the other side
    With all their grapplers.   Swift their flight was ta'en.
Down to the place from either hand they glide,
    Reaching their hooks to those who were limed fast,
    And now beneath the scum were being fried.   150
And from them thus engaged we onward passed.

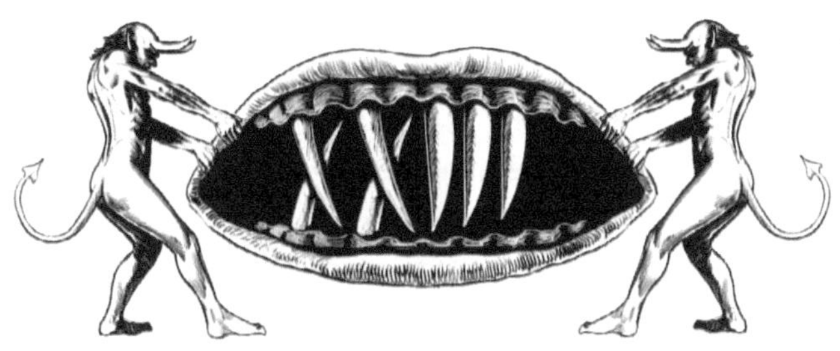

The Eighth Circle ❧ escape from the Fifth to the Sixth Bolgia, where the Hypocrites walk at a snail's
pace, weighed down by Gilded Cloaks of lead ❧ the Merry Friars Catalano and Loderingo ❧ Caiaphas

SILENT, ALONE, not now with company
 We onward went, one first and one behind,
 As Minor Friars use to make their way.
On Æsop's fable wholly was my mind
 Intent, by reason of that contest new—
 The fable where the frog and mouse we find ;
For *Mo* and *Issa* are not more of hue
 Than like the fable shall the fact appear,
 If but considered with attention due.
And as from one thought springs the next, so here   10
 Out of my first arose another thought,
 Until within me doubled was my fear.
For thus I judged : Seeing through us were brought
 Contempt upon them, hurt, and sore despite,
 They needs must be to deep vexation wrought.
If anger to malevolence unite,
 Then will they us more cruelly pursue
 Than dog the hare which almost feels its bite.
All my hair bristled, I already knew,
 With terror when I spake : ' O Master, try   20
 To hide us quick' (and back I turned to view
What lay behind), ' for me they terrify,
 These Malebranche following us ; from dread
 I almost fancy I can feel them nigh.'
And he : ' Were I a mirror backed with lead
 I should no truer glass that form of thine,
 Than all thy thought by mine is answered.
For even now thy thoughts accord with mine,
 Alike in drift and featured with one face ;
 And to suggest one counsel they combine.   30

If the right bank slope downward at this place,
    To the next Bolgia offering us a way,
    Swiftly shall we evade the imagined chase.'
Ere he completely could his purpose say,
    I saw them with their wings extended wide,
    Close on us ; as of us to make their prey.
Then quickly was I snatched up by my Guide :
    Even as a mother when, awaked by cries,
    She sees the flames are kindling at her side,
Delaying not, seizes her child and flies ;   40
    Careful for him her proper danger mocks,
    Nor even with one poor shift herself supplies.
And he, stretched out upon the flinty rocks,
    Himself unto the precipice resigned
    Which one side of the other Bolgia blocks.
A swifter course ne'er held a stream confined,
    That it may turn a mill, within its race,
    Where near the buckets 'tis the most declined
Than was my Master's down that rock's sheer face ;
    Nor seemed I then his comrade, as we sped,   50
    But like a son locked in a sire's embrace.
And barely had his feet struck on the bed
    Of the low ground, when they were seen to stand
    Upon the crest, no more a cause of dread.
For Providence supreme, who so had planned
    In the Fifth Bolgia they should minister,
    Them wholly from departure thence had banned.
'neath us we saw a painted people fare,
    Weeping as on their way they circled slow,
    Crushed by fatigue to look at, and despair.   60
Cloaks had they on with hoods pulled down full low
    Upon their eyes, and fashioned, as it seemed,
    Like those which at Cologne for monks they sew.
The outer face was gilt so that it gleamed ;
    Inside was all of lead, of such a weight
    Frederick's to these had been but straw esteemed.
O weary robes for an eternal state !
    With them we turned to the left hand once more,
    Intent upon their tears disconsolate.

But those folk, wearied with the loads they bore,   70
    So slowly crept that still new company
    Was ours at every footfall on the floor.
Whence to my Guide I said :   ' Do thou now try
    To find some one by name or action known,
    And as we go on all sides turn thine eye.'
And one, who recognised the Tuscan tone,
    Called from behind us :   ' Halt, I you entreat
    Who through the air obscure are hastening on ;
Haply in me thou what thou seek'st shalt meet.'
    Whereon my Guide turned round and said :   ' Await,   80
    And keep thou time with pacing of his feet.'
I stood, and saw two manifesting great
    Desire to join me, by their countenance ;
    But their loads hampered them and passage strait.
And, when arrived, me with an eye askance
    They gazed on long time, but no word they spoke ;
    Then, to each other turned, held thus parlance :
' His heaving throat proves him of living folk.
    If they are of the dead, how could they gain
    To walk uncovered by the heavy cloak ?'   90
Then to me :   ' Tuscan, who dost now attain
    To the college of the hypocrites forlorn,
    To tell us who thou art show no disdain.'
And I to them :   ' I was both bred and born
    In the great city by fair Arno's stream,
    And wear the body I have always worn.
But who are ye, whose suffering supreme
    Makes tears, as I behold, to flood the cheek ;
    And what your mode of pain that thus doth gleam ?'
' Ah me, the yellow mantles,' one to speak   100
    Began, ' are all of lead so thick, its weight
    Maketh the scales after this manner creak.
We, Merry Friars of Bologna's state,
    I Catalano, Loderingo he,
    Were by thy town together designate,
As for the most part one is used to be,
    To keep the peace within it ; and around
    Gardingo, what we were men still may see.'

CAIAPHAS
Canto XXIII, lines 124 - 148

I made beginning :   ' Friars, your profound—'
    But said no more, on suddenly seeing there   110
    One crucified by three stakes to the ground,
Who, when he saw me, writhed as in despair,
    Breathing into his beard with heavy sigh.
    And Friar Catalan, of this aware,
Said :   ' He thus fixed, on whom thou turn'st thine eye,
    Counselled the Pharisees that it behoved
    One man as victim for the folk should die.
Naked, thou seest, he lies, and ne'er removed
    From where, set 'cross the path, by him the weight
    Of every one that passes by is proved.   120
And his wife's father shares an equal fate,
    With others of the Council, in this fosse ;
    For to the Jews they proved seed reprobate.'
Meanwhile at him thus stretched upon the cross
    Virgil, I saw, displayed astonishment—
    At his mean exile and eternal loss.
And then this question to the Friars he sent :
    ' Be not displeased, but, if ye may, avow
    If on the right hand there lies any vent
By which we, both of us, from hence may go,   130
    Nor need the black angelic company
    To come to help us from this valley low.'
' Nearer than what thou think'st,' he made reply,
    ' A rib there runs from the encircling wall,
    The cruel vales in turn o'erarching high ;
Save that at this 'tis rent and ruined all.
    Ye can climb upward o'er the shattered heap
    Where down the side the piled-up fragments fall.'
His head bent down a while my Guide did keep,
    Then said :   ' He warned us in imperfect wise,   140
    Who sinners with his hook doth clutch and steep.'
The Friar :   ' At Bologna many a vice
    I heard the Devil charged with, and among
    The rest that, false, he father is of lies.'
Then onward moved my Guide with paces long,
    And some slight shade of anger on his face.
    I with him parted from the burdened throng,
Stepping where those dear feet had left their trace.

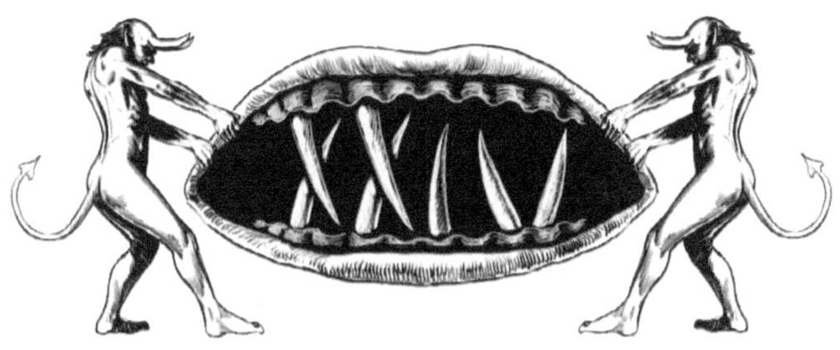

The Eighth Circle ❧ *arduous passage over the cliff into the Seventh Bolgia, where the Thieves are tormented by Serpents, and are constantly undergoing a hideous metamorphosis* ❧ *Vanni Fucci*

IN SEASON OF THE NEW YEAR, when the sun
    Beneath Aquarius warms again his hair,
    And somewhat on the nights the days have won ;
When on the ground the hoar-frost painteth fair
    A mimic image of her sister white—
    But soon her brush of colour is all bare—
The clown, whose fodder is consumed outright,
    Rises and looks abroad, and, all the plain
    Beholding glisten, on his thigh doth smite.
Returned indoors, like wretch that seeks in vain   10
    What he should do, restless he mourns his case ;
    But hope revives when, looking forth again,
He sees the earth anew has changed its face.
    Then with his crook he doth himself provide,
    And straightway doth his sheep to pasture chase :
So at my Master was I terrified,
    His brows beholding troubled ; nor more slow
    To where I ailed the plaster was applied.
For when the broken bridge we stood below
    My Guide turned to me with the expression sweet   20
    Which I beneath the mountain learned to know.
His arms he opened, after counsel meet
    Held with himself, and, scanning closely o'er
    The fragments first, he raised me from my feet ;
And like a man who, working, looks before,
    With foresight still on that in front bestowed,
    Me to the summit of a block he bore
And then to me another fragment showed,
    Saying : ' By this thou now must clamber on ;
    But try it first if it will bear thy load.'   30

The heavy cowled this way could ne'er have gone,
    For hardly we, I holpen, he so light,
    Could clamber up from shattered stone to stone.
And but that on the inner bank the height
    Of wall is not so great, I say not he,
    But for myself I had been vanquished quite.
But Malebolge to the cavity
    Of the deep central pit is planned to fall ;
    Hence every Bolgia in its turn must be
High on the out, low on the inner wall ;   40
    So to the summit we attained at last,
    Whence breaks away the topmost stone of all.
My lungs were so with breathlessness harassed,
    The summit won, I could no further go ;
    And, hardly there, me on the ground I cast
' Well it befits that thou shouldst from thee throw
    All sloth,' the Master said ; ' for stretched in down
    Or under awnings none can glory know.
And he who spends his life nor wins renown
    Leaves in the world no more enduring trace   50
    Than smoke in air, or foam on water blown.
Therefore arise ; o'ercome thy breathlessness
    By force of will, victor in every fight
    When not subservient to the body base.
Of stairs thou yet must climb a loftier flight :
    'Tis not enough to have ascended these.
    Up then and profit if thou hear'st aright.'
Rising I feigned to breathe with greater ease
    Than what I felt, and spake :   ' Now forward plod,
    For with my courage now my strength agrees.'   60
Up o'er the rocky rib we held our road ;
    And rough it was and difficult and strait,
    And steeper far than that we earlier trod.
Speaking I went, to hide my wearied state,
    When from the neighbouring moat a voice we heard
    Which seemed ill fitted to articulate.
Of what it said I knew not any word,
    Though on the arch that vaults the moat set high ;
    But he who spake appeared by anger stirred.

Though I bent downward yet my eager eye,   70
    So dim the depth, explored it all in vain ;
    I then :   ' O Master, to that bank draw nigh,
And let us by the wall descent obtain,
    Because I hear and do not understand,
    And looking down distinguish nothing plain.'
' My sole reply to thee,' he answered bland,
    ' Is to perform ; for it behoves,' he said,
    ' With silent act to answer just demand.'
Then we descended from the bridge's head,
    Where with the eighth bank is its junction wrought ;   80
    And full beneath me was the Bolgia spread.
And I perceived that hideously 'twas fraught
    With serpents ; and such monstrous forms they bore,
    Even now my blood is curdled at the thought.
Henceforth let sandy Libya boast no more !
    Though she breed hydra, snake that crawls or flies,
    Twy-headed, or fine-speckled, no such store
Of plagues, nor near so cruel, she supplies,
    Though joined to all the land of Ethiop,
    And that which by the Red Sea waters lies.   90
'midst this fell throng and dismal, without hope
    A naked people ran, aghast with fear—
    No covert for them and no heliotrope.
Their hands were bound by serpents at their rear,
    Which in their reins for head and tail did get
    A holding-place : in front they knotted were.
And lo ! to one who on our side was set
    A serpent darted forward, him to bite
    At where the neck is by the shoulders met.
Nor *O* nor *I* did any ever write   100
    More quickly than he kindled, burst in flame,
    And crumbled all to ashes.   And when quite
He on the earth a wasted heap became,
    The ashes of themselves together rolled,
    Resuming suddenly their former frame.
Thus, as by mighty sages we are told,
    The Phoenix dies, and then is born again,
    When it is close upon five centuries old.

THE SERPENTS
Canto XXIV, lines 67 - 118

In all its life it eats not herb nor grain,
    But only tears that from frankincense flow ;   110
    It, for a shroud, sweet nard and myrrh contain.
And as the man who falls and knows not how,
    By force of demons stretched upon the ground,
    Or by obstruction that makes life run low,
When risen up straight gazes all around
    In deep confusion through the anguish keen
    He suffered from, and stares with sighs profound :
So was the sinner, when arisen, seen.
    Justice of God, how are thy terrors piled,
    Showering in vengeance blows thus big with teen !   120
My Guide then asked of him how he was styled.
    Whereon he said :   ' From Tuscany I rained,
    Not long ago, into this gullet wild.
From bestial life, not human, joy I gained,
    Mule that I was ; me, Vanni Fucci, brute,
    Pistoia, fitting den, in life contained.'
I to my Guide :   ' Bid him not budge a foot,
    And ask what crime has plunged him here below.
    In rage and blood I knew him dissolute.'
The sinner heard, nor insincere did show,   130
    But towards me turned his face and eke his mind,
    With spiteful shame his features all aglow ;
Then said :   ' It pains me more thou shouldst me find
    And catch me steeped in all this misery,
    Than when the other life I left behind.
What thou demandest I can not deny :
    I'm plunged thus low because the thief I played
    Within the fairly furnished sacristy ;
And falsely to another's charge 'twas laid.
    Lest thou shouldst joy such sight has met thy view   140
    If e'er these dreary regions thou evade,
Give ear and hearken to my utterance true :
    The Neri first out of Pistoia fail,
    Her laws and parties Florence shapes anew ;

Mars draws a vapour out of Magra's vale,
    Which black and threatening clouds accompany :
    Then bursting in a tempest terrible
Upon Piceno shall the war run high ;
    The mist by it shall suddenly be rent,
    And every Bianco smitten be thereby   150
And I have told thee that thou mayst lament.'

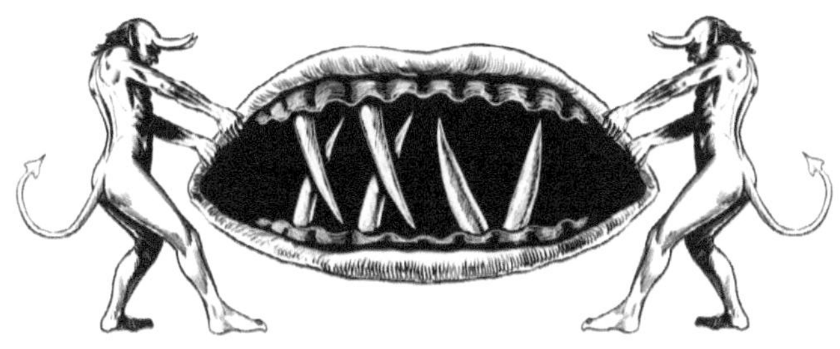

The Eighth Circle ❧ Seventh Bolgia continued ❧ Cacus ❧ Agnello Brunelleschi,
Buoso degli Abati, Puccio Sciancato, Cianfa Donati, and Guercio Cavalcanti

THE ROBBER, when his words were ended so,
    Made both the figs and lifted either fist,
    Shouting :   ' There, God ! For them at thee I throw.'
Then were the snakes my friends ; for one 'gan twist
    And coiled itself around the sinner's throat,
    As if to say :   ' Now would I have thee whist.'
Another seized his arms and made a knot,
    Clinching itself upon them in such wise
    He had no power to move them by a jot.
Pistoia ! thou, Pistoia, shouldst devise   10
    To burn thyself to ashes, since thou hast
    Outrun thy founders in iniquities.
The blackest depths of Hell through which I passed
    Showed me no soul 'gainst God so filled with spite,
    No, not even he who down Thebes' wall was cast.
He spake no further word, but turned to flight ;
    And I beheld a Centaur raging sore
    Come shouting :   ' Of the ribald give me sight !'
I scarce believe Maremma yieldeth more
    Snakes of all kinds than what composed the load   20
    Which on his back, far as our form, he bore.
Behind his nape, with pinions spread abroad,
    A dragon couchant on his shoulders lay
    To set on fire whoever bars his road.
' This one is Cacus,' did my Master say,
    ' Who underneath the rock of Aventine
    Watered a pool with blood day after day.
Not with his brethren runs he in the line,
    Because of yore the treacherous theft he wrought
    Upon the neighbouring wealthy herd of kine :   30

Whence to his crooked course an end was brought
    'Neath Hercules' club, which on him might shower down
    A hundred blows ; ere ten he suffered nought.'
While this he said, the other had passed on ;
    And under us three spirits forward pressed
    Of whom my Guide and I had nothing known
But that :   ' Who are ye ?' They made loud request.
    Whereon our tale no further could proceed ;
    And toward them wholly we our wits addressed.
I recognised them not, but gave good heed ;   40
    Till, as it often haps in such a case,
    To name another, one discovered need,
Saying :   ' Now where stopped Cianfa in the race ?'
    Then, that my Guide might halt and hearken well,
    On chin and nose I did my finger place.
If, Reader, to believe what now I tell
    Thou shouldst be slow, I wonder not, for I
    Who saw it all scarce find it credible.
While I on them my brows kept lifted high
    A serpent, which had six feet, suddenly flew   50
    At one of them and held him bodily.
Its middle feet about his paunch it drew,
    And with the two in front his arms clutched fast,
    And bit one cheek and the other through and through.
Its hinder feet upon his thighs it cast,
    Thrusting its tail between them till behind,
    Distended o'er his reins, it upward passed.
The ivy to a tree could never bind
    Itself so firmly as this dreadful beast
    Its members with the other's intertwined.   60
Each lost the colour that it once possessed,
    And closely they, like heated wax, unite,
    The former hue of neither manifest :
Even so up o'er papyrus, when alight,
    Before the flame there spreads a colour dun,
    Not black as yet, though from it dies the white.
The other two meanwhile were looking on,
    Crying :   ' Agnello, how art thou made new !
    Thou art not twain, and yet no longer one.'

FUCCI AND CACUS
Canto XXV, lines 1 - 151

A single head was moulded out of two ;   70
    And on our sight a single face arose,
    Which out of both lost countenances grew.
Four separate limbs did but two arms compose ;
    Belly with chest, and legs with thighs did grow
    To members such as nought created shows.
Their former fashion was all perished now :
    The perverse shape did both, yet neither seem ;
    And, thus transformed, departed moving slow.
And as the lizard, which at fierce extreme
    Of dog-day heat another hedge would gain,   80
    Flits 'cross the path swift as the lightning's gleam ;
Right for the bellies of the other twain
    A little snake quivering with anger sped,
    Livid and black as is a pepper grain,
And on the part by which we first are fed
    Pierced one of them ; and then upon the ground
    It fell before him, and remained outspread.
The wounded gazed on it, but made no sound.
    Rooted he stood and yawning, scarce awake,
    As seized by fever or by sleep profound.   90
It closely watched him and he watched the snake,
    While from its mouth and from his wound 'gan swell
    Volumes of smoke which joined one cloud to make.
Be Lucan henceforth dumb, nor longer tell
    Of plagued Sabellus and Nassidius,
    But, hearkening to what follows, mark it well.
Silent be Ovid : of him telling us
    How Cadmus to a snake, and to a fount
    Changed Arethuse, I am not envious ;
For never of two natures front to front   100
    In metamorphosis, while mutually
    The forms their matter changed, he gives account.
'Twas thus that each to the other made reply :
    Its tail into a fork the serpent split ;
    Bracing his feet the other pulled them nigh :
And then in one so thoroughly were knit
    His legs and thighs, no searching could divine
    At where the junction had been wrought in it.

The shape, of which the one lost every sign,
 The cloven tail was taking ; then the skin   110
 Of one grew rough, the other's soft and fine.
I by the armpits saw the arms drawn in ;
 And now the monster's feet, which had been small,
 What the other's lost in length appeared to win.
Together twisted, its hind feet did fall
 And grew the member men are used to hide :
 For his the wretch gained feet with which to crawl.
Dyed in the smoke they took on either side
 A novel colour : hair unwonted grew
 On one ; the hair upon the other died   120
The one fell prone, erect the other drew,
 With cruel eyes continuing to glare,
 'Neath which their muzzles metamorphose knew.
The erect to his brows drew his. Of stuff to spare
 Of what he upward pulled, there was no lack ;
 So ears were formed on cheeks that erst were bare.
Of that which clung in front nor was drawn back,
 Superfluous, on the face was formed a nose,
 And lips absorbed the skin that still was slack.
His muzzle who lay prone now forward goes ;   130
 Backward into his head his ears he draws
 Even as a snail appears its horns to lose.
The tongue, which had been whole and ready was
 For speech, cleaves now ; the forked tongue of the snake
 Joins in the other : and the smoke has pause.
The soul which thus a brutish form did take,
 Along the valley, hissing, swiftly fled ;
 The other close behind it spluttering spake,
Then, toward it turning his new shoulders, said
 Unto the third : ' Now Buoso down the way   140
 May hasten crawling, as I earlier sped.'
Ballast which in the Seventh Bolgia lay
 Thus saw I shift and change. Be my excuse
 The novel theme, if swerves my pen astray.
And though these things mine eyesight might confuse
 A little, and my mind with fear divide,
 Such secrecy they fleeing could not use

But that Puccio Sciancatto plain I spied ;
    And he alone of the companions three
    Who came at first, was left unmodified.   150
For the other, tears, Gaville, are shed by thee.

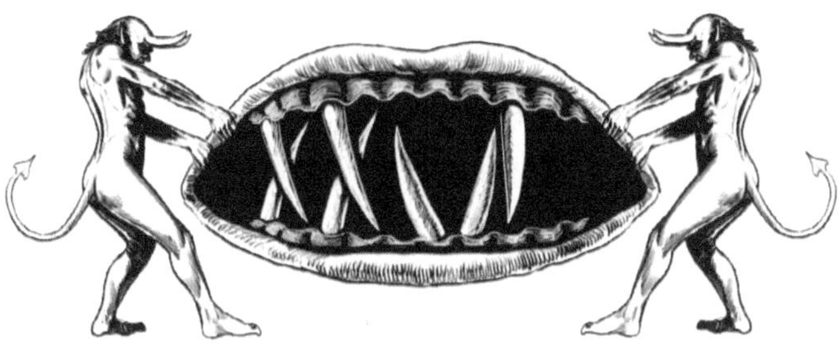

The Eighth Circle ✿ *Eighth Bolgia, where are the Evil Counsellors, wrapped
each in his own Flame* ✿ *Ulysses tells how he met with death*

REJOICE, O FLORENCE, in thy widening fame !
 Thy wings thou beatest over land and sea,
 And even through Inferno spreads thy name.
Burghers of thine, five such were found by me
 Among the thieves ; whence I ashamed grew,
 Nor shall great glory thence redound to thee.
But if 'tis toward the morning dreams are true,
 Thou shalt experience ere long time be gone
 The doom even Prato prays for as thy due.
And came it now, it would not come too soon.   10
 Would it were come as come it must with time :
 ' Twill crush me more the older I am grown.
Departing thence, my Guide began to climb
 The jutting rocks by which we made descent
 Some while ago, and pulled me after him.
And as upon our lonely way we went
 'Mong splinters of the cliff, the feet in vain,
 Without the hand to help, had labour spent.
I sorrowed, and am sorrow-smit again,
 Recalling what before mine eyes there lay,   20
 And, more than I am wont, my genius rein
From running save where virtue leads the way ;
 So that if happy star or holier might
 Have gifted me I never mourn it may.
At time of year when he who gives earth light
 His face shows to us longest visible,
 When gnats replace the fly at fall of night,
Not by the peasant resting on the hill
 Are seen more fire-flies in the vale below,
 Where he perchance doth field and vineyard till,   30

Than flamelets I beheld resplendent glow
    Throughout the whole Eighth Bolgia, when at last
    I stood whence I the bottom plain could know.
And as he whom the bears avenged, when passed
    From the earth Elijah, saw the chariot rise
    With horses heavenward reared and mounting fast,
And no long time had traced it with his eyes
    Till but a flash of light it all became,
    Which like a rack of cloud swept to the skies :
Deep in the valley's gorge, in mode the same,   40
    These flitted ; what it held by none was shown,
    And yet a sinner lurked in every flame.
To see them well I from the bridge peered down,
    And if a jutting crag I had not caught
    I must have fallen, though neither thrust nor thrown.
My Leader me beholding lost in thought :
    ' In all the fires are spirits,' said to me ;
    ' His flame round each is for a garment wrought.'
' O Master !'   I replied, ' by hearing thee
    I grow assured, but yet I knew before   50
    That thus indeed it was, and longed to be
Told who is in the flame which there doth soar,
    Cloven, as if ascending from the pyre
    Where with Eteocles there burned of yore
His brother.'   He :   ' Ulysses in that fire
    And Diomedes burn ; in punishment
    Thus held together, as they held in ire.
And, wrapped within their flame, they now repent
    The ambush of the horse, which oped the door
    Through which the Romans' noble seed forth went.   60
For guile Deïdamia makes deplore
    In death her lost Achilles, tears they shed,
    And bear for the Palladium vengeance sore.'
' Master, I pray thee fervently,' I said,
    ' If from those flames they still can utter speech—
    Give ear as if a thousand times I pled !
Refuse not here to linger, I beseech,
    Until the cloven fire shall hither gain :
    Thou seest how toward it eagerly I reach.'

And he :   'Thy prayers are worthy to obtain   70
       Exceeding praise ; thou hast what thou dost seek :
       But see that thou from speech thy tongue refrain.
I know what thou wouldst have ; leave me to speak,
       For they perchance would hear contemptuously
       Shouldst thou address them, seeing they were Greek.'
Soon as the flame toward us had come so nigh
       That to my Leader time and place seemed met,
       I heard him thus adjure it to reply :
' O ye who twain within one fire are set,
       If what I did your guerdon meriteth,   80
       If much or little ye are in my debt
For the great verse I built while I had breath,
       By one of you be openly confessed
       Where, lost to men, at last he met with death.'
Of the ancient flame the more conspicuous crest
       Murmuring began to waver up and down
       Like flame that flickers, by the wind distressed.
At length by it was measured motion shown,
       Like tongue that moves in speech ; and by the flame
       Was language uttered thus :   'When I had gone   90
From Circe who a long year kept me tame
       Beside her, ere the near Gaeta had
       Receivèd from Æneas that new name ;
No softness for my son, nor reverence sad
       For my old father, nor the love I owed
       Penelope with which to make her glad,
Could quench the ardour that within me glowed
       A full experience of the world to gain—
       Of human vice and worth.   But I abroad
Launched out upon the high and open main   100
       With but one bark and but the little band
       Which ne'er deserted me.   As far as Spain
I saw the sea-shore upon either hand,
       And as Morocco ; saw Sardinia's isle,
       And all of which those waters wash the strand.
I and my comrades were grown old the while
       And sluggish, ere we to the narrows came
       Where Hercules of old did landmarks pile

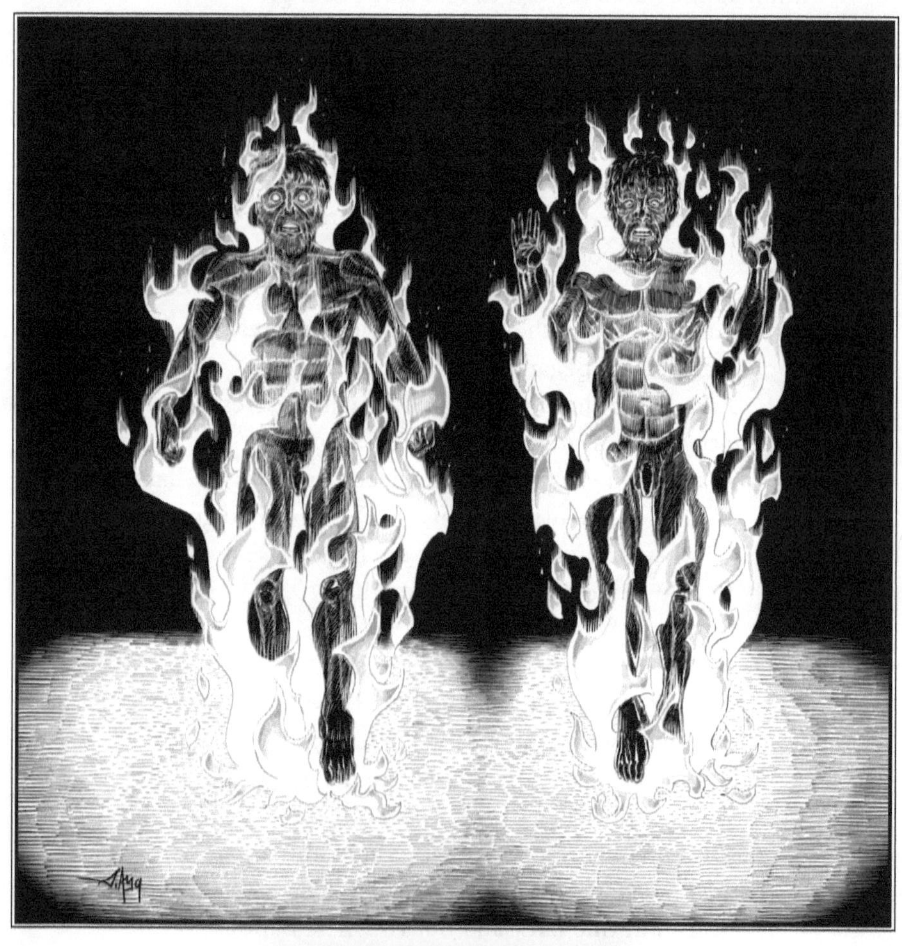

ULYSSESS AND DIOMEDE
Canto XXVI, lines 85 - 142

For sign to men they should no further aim ;
    And Seville lay behind me on the right,   110
    As on the left lay Ceuta.   Then to them
I spake :   " O Brothers, who through such a fight
    Of hundred thousand dangers West have won,
    In this short watch that ushers in the night
Of all your senses, ere your day be done,
    Refuse not to obtain experience new
    Of worlds unpeopled, yonder, past the sun.
Consider whence the seed of life ye drew ;
    Ye were not born to live like brutish herd,
    But righteousness and wisdom to ensue."   120
My comrades to such eagerness were stirred
    By this short speech the course to enter on,
    They had no longer brooked restraining word.
Turning our poop to where the morning shone
    We of the oars made wings for our mad flight,
    Still tending left the further we had gone.
And of the other pole I saw at night
    Now all the stars ; and 'neath the watery plain
    Our own familiar heavens were lost to sight.
Five times afresh had kindled, and again   130
    The moon's face earthward was illumed no more,
    Since out we sailed upon the mighty main ;
Then we beheld a lofty mountain soar,
    Dim in the distance ; higher, as I thought,
    By far than any I had seen before.
We joyed ; but with despair were soon distraught
    When burst a whirlwind from the new-found world
    And the forequarter of the vessel caught.
With all the waters thrice it round was swirled ;
    At the fourth time the poop, heaved upward, rose,   140
    The prow, as pleased Another, down was hurled ;
And then above us did the ocean close.'

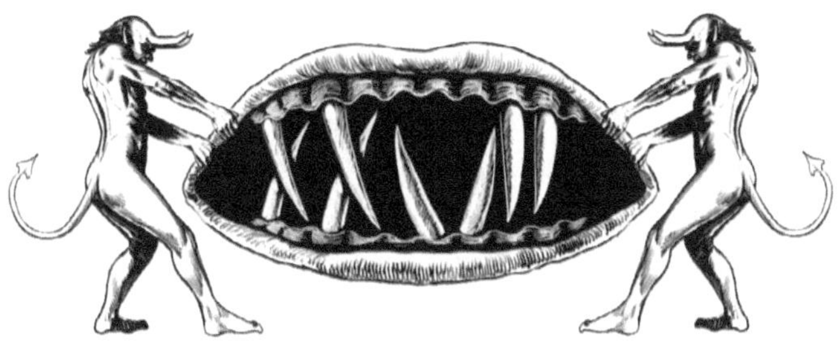

*The Eighth Circle ∾ Eighth Bolgia continued ∾ Guido of Montefeltro
∾ the Cities of Romagna ∾ Guido and Boniface VIII.*

NOW, HAVING FIRST ERECT and silent grown
    (For it would say no more), from us the flame,
    The Poet sweet consenting, had moved on ;
And then our eyes were turned to one that came
    Behind it on the way, by sounds that burst
    Out of its crest in a confusèd stream.
As the Sicilian bull, which bellowed first
    With his lamenting—and it was but right—
    Who had prepared it with his tools accurst,
Roared with the howlings of the tortured wight,   10
    So that although constructed all of brass
    Yet seemed it pierced with anguish to the height ;
So, wanting road and vent by which to pass
    Up through the flame, into the flame's own speech
    The woeful language all converted was.
But when the words at length contrived to reach
    The top, while hither thither shook the crest
    As moved the tongue at utterance of each,
We heard :   ' Oh thou, to whom are now addressed
    My words, who spakest now in Lombard phrase :   20
    " Depart ; of thee I nothing more request."
Though I be late arrived, yet of thy grace
    Let it not irk thee here a while to stay :
    It irks not me, yet, as thou seest, I blaze.
If lately to this world devoid of day
    From that sweet Latian land thou art come down
    Whence all my guilt I bring, declare and say
Has now Romagna peace ? because my own
    Native abode was in the mountain land
    'Tween springs of Tiber and Urbino town.'   30

While I intent and bending low did stand,
    My Leader, as he touched me on the side,
     ' Speak thou, for he is Latian,' gave command.
Whereon without delay I thus replied—
    Because already was my speech prepared :
     ' Soul, that down there dost in concealment 'bide,
In thy Romagna wars have never spared
    And spare not now in tyrants' hearts to rage ;
     But when I left it there was none declared.
No change has fallen Ravenna for an age.   40
    There, covering Cervia too with outspread wing,
     Polenta's Eagle guards his heritage.
Over the city which long suffering
    Endured, and Frenchmen slain on Frenchmen rolled,
     The Green Paws once again protection fling.
The Mastiffs of Verrucchio, young and old,
    Who to Montagna brought such evil cheer,
     Still clinch their fangs where they were wont to hold.
Cities, Lamone and Santerno near,
    The Lion couched in white are governed by   50
     Which changes party with the changing year.
And that to which the Savio wanders nigh
    As it is set 'twixt mountain and champaign
     Lives now in freedom now 'neath tyranny.
But who thou art I to be told am fain :
    Be not more stubborn than we others found,
     As thou on earth illustrious wouldst remain.'
When first the fire a little while had moaned
    After its manner, next the pointed crest
     Waved to and fro ; then in this sense breathed sound : 60
' If I believed my answer were addressed
    To one that earthward shall his course retrace,
     This flame should forthwith altogether rest.
But since none ever yet out of this place
    Returned alive, if all be true I hear,
     I yield thee answer fearless of disgrace.
I was a warrior, then a Cordelier ;
    Thinking thus girt to purge away my stain :
     And sure my hope had met with answer clear

Had not the High Priest—ill with him remain ! 70
    Plunged me anew into my former sin :
    And why and how, I would to thee make plain.
While I the frame of bones and flesh was in
    My mother gave me, all the deeds I wrought
    Were fox-like and in no wise leonine.
Of every wile and hidden way I caught
    The secret trick, and used them with such sleight
    That all the world with fame of it was fraught.
When I perceived I had attainèd quite
    The time of life when it behoves each one 80
    To furl his sails and coil his cordage tight,
Sorrowing for deeds I had with pleasure done,
    Contrite and shriven, I religious grew.
    Ah, wretched me ! and well it was begun
But for the Chieftain of the Pharisees new,
    Then waging war hard by the Lateran,
    And not with Saracen nor yet with Jew ;
For Christian were his enemies every man,
    And none had at the siege of Acre been
    Or trafficked in the Empire of Soldàn. 90
His lofty office he held cheap, and e'en
    His Sacred Orders and the cord I wore,
    Which used to make the wearers of it lean.
As from Soracte Constantine of yore
    Sylvester called to cure his leprosy,
    I as a leech was called this man before
To cure him of his fever which ran high ;
    My counsel he required, but I stood dumb,
    For drunken all his words appeared to be.
He said ; " For fear be in thy heart no room ; 100
    Beforehand I absolve thee, but declare
    How Palestrina I may overcome.
Heaven I unlock, as thou art well aware,
    And close at will ; because the keys are twin
    My predecessor was averse to bear."
Then did his weighty reasoning on me win
    Till to be silent seemed the worst of all ;
    And, " Father," I replied, " since from this sin

THE GUIDO OF MONTEFELTRO
Canto XXVII, lines 112 - 127

Thou dost absolve me into which I fall—
    The scant performance of a promise wide 110
    Will yield thee triumph in thy lofty stall."
Francis came for me soon as e'er I died ;
    But one of the black Cherubim was there
    And " Take him not, nor rob me of him " cried,
" For him of right among my thralls I bear
    Because he offered counsel fraudulent ;
    Since when I've had him firmly by the hair.
None is absolved unless he first repent ;
    Nor can repentance house with purpose ill,
    For this the contradiction doth prevent." 120
Ah, wretched me !   How did I shrinking thrill
    When clutching me he sneered :   " Perhaps of old
    Thou didst not think I had in logic skill."
He carried me to Minos : Minos rolled
    His tail eight times round his hard back ; in ire
    Biting it fiercely, ere of me he told :
" Among the sinners of the shrouding fire !"
    Therefore am I, where thou beholdest, lost ;
    And, sore at heart, go clothed in such attire.'
What he would say thus ended by the ghost, 130
    Away from us the moaning flame did glide
    While to and fro its pointed horn was tossed.
But we passed further on, I and my Guide,
    Along the cliff to where the arch is set
    O'er the next moat, where paying they reside,
As schismatics who whelmed themselves in debt.

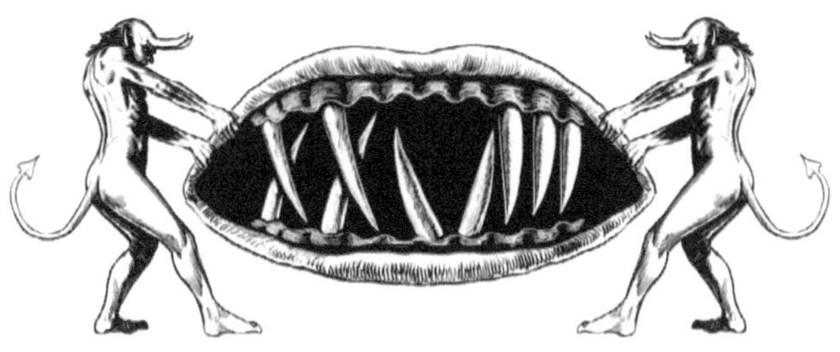

COULD ANY, even in words unclogged by rhyme
    Recount the wounds that now I saw, and blood,
    Although he aimed at it time after time ?
Here every tongue must fail of what it would,
    Because our human speech and powers of thought
    To grasp so much come short in aptitude.
If all the people were together brought
    Who in Apulia, land distressed by fate,
    Made lamentation for the bloodshed wrought
By Rome ; and in that war procrastinate   10
    When the large booty of the rings was won,
    As Livy writes whose every word has weight ;
With those on whom such direful deeds were done
    When Robert Guiscard they as foes assailed ;
    And those of whom still turns up many a bone
At Ceperan, where each Apulian failed
    In faith ; and those at Tagliacozzo strewed,
    Where old Alardo, not by arms, prevailed ;
And each his wounds and mutilations showed,
    Yet would they far behind by those be left   20
    Who had the vile Ninth Bolgia for abode.
No cask, of middle stave or end bereft,
    E'er gaped like one I saw the rest among,
    Slit from the chin all downward to the cleft.
Between his legs his entrails drooping hung ;
    The pluck and that foul bag were evident
    Which changes what is swallowed into dung.
And while I gazed upon him all intent,
    Opening his breast his eyes on me he set,
    Saying : ' Behold, how by myself I'm rent !   30

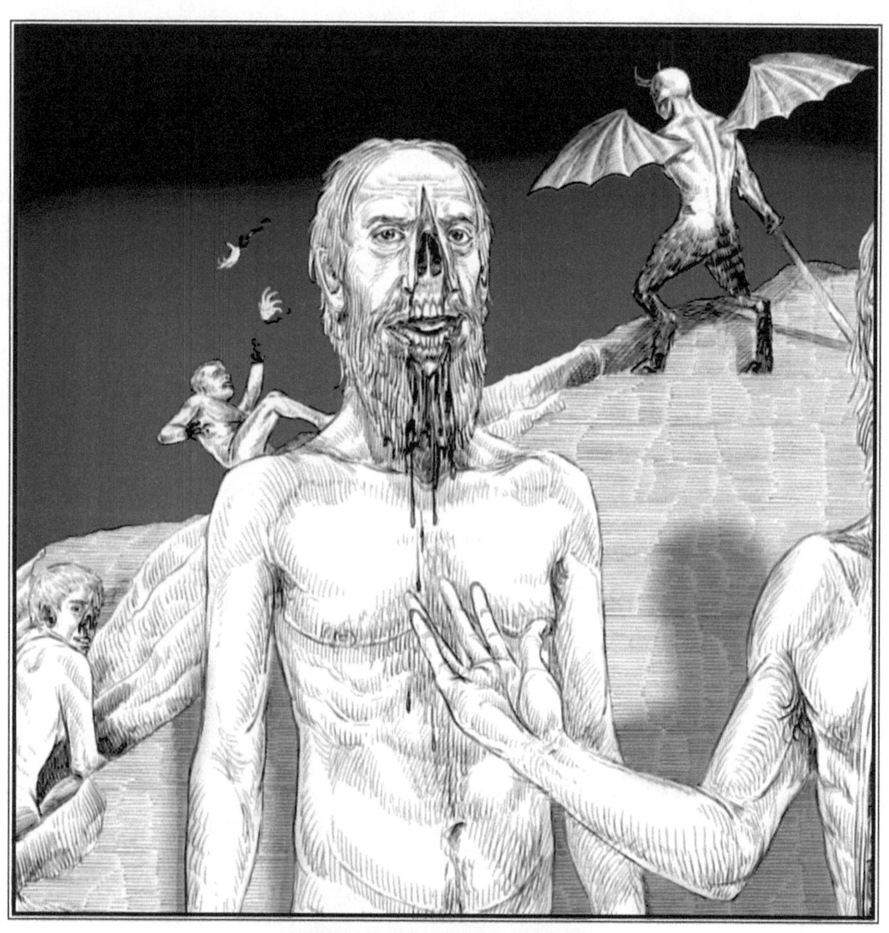

SCHISMATICS
Canto XXVIII, lines 25 - 49

See how dismembered now is Mahomet !
    Ali in front of me goes weeping too ;
    With visage from the chin to forelock split.
By all the others whom thou seest there grew
    Scandal and schism while yet they breathed the day ;
    Because of which they now are cloven through.
There stands behind a devil on the way,
    Us with his sword thus cruelly to trim :
    He cleaves again each of our company
As soon as we complete the circuit grim ;   40
    Because the wounds of each are healed outright
    Or e'er anew he goes in front of him.
But who art thou that peerest from the height,
    It may be putting off to reach the pain
    Which shall the crimes confessed by thee requite ?'
' Death has not seized him yet, nor is he ta'en
    To torment for his sins,' my Master said ;
    ' But, that he may a full experience gain,
By me, a ghost, 'tis doomed he should be led
    Down the Infernal circles, round on round ;   50
    And what I tell thee is the truth indeed.'
A hundred shades and more, to whom the sound
    Had reached, stood in the moat to mark me well,
    Their pangs forgot ; so did the words astound.
' Let Fra Dolcin provide, thou mayst him tell—
    Thou, who perchance ere long shalt sunward go—
    Unless he soon would join me in this Hell,
Much food, lest aided by the siege of snow
    The Novarese should o'er him victory get,
    Which otherwise to win they would be slow.'   60
While this was said to me by Mahomet
    One foot he held uplifted ; to the ground
    He let it fall, and so he forward set
Next, one whose throat was gaping with a wound,
    Whose nose up to the brows away was sheared
    And on whose head a single ear was found,
At me, with all the others, wondering peered ;
    And, ere the rest, an open windpipe made,
    The outside of it all with crimson smeared.

THE NINTH GULF
Canto XXVIII, lines 91 - 106

'O thou, not here because of guilt,' he said ;   70
    'And whom I sure on Latian ground did know
    Unless by strong similitude betrayed,
Upon Pier da Medicin bestow
    A thought, shouldst thou revisit the sweet plain
    That from Vercelli slopes to Marcabò.
And make thou known to Fano's worthiest twain—
    To Messer Guido and to Angiolel—
    They, unless foresight here be wholly vain,
Thrown overboard in gyve and manacle
    Shall drown fast by Cattolica, as planned   80
    By treachery of a tyrant fierce and fell.
Between Majolica and Cyprus strand
    A blacker crime did Neptune never spy
    By pirates wrought, or even by Argives' hand.
The traitor who is blinded of an eye,
    Lord of the town which of my comrades one
    Had been far happier ne'er to have come nigh,
To parley with him will allure them on,
    Then so provide, against Focara's blast
    No need for them of vow or orison.'   90
And I : 'Point out and tell, if wish thou hast
    To get news of thee to the world conveyed,
    Who rues that e'er his eyes thereon were cast ?'
On a companion's jaw his hand he laid,
    And shouted, while the mouth he open prised :
    ' 'Tis this one here by whom no word is said.
He quenched all doubt in Cæsar, and advised—
    Himself an outlaw—that a man equipped
    For strife ran danger if he temporised.'
Alas, to look on, how downcast and hipped   100
    Curio, once bold in counsel, now appeared ;
    With gorge whence by the roots the tongue was ripped.
Another one, whose hands away were sheared,
    In the dim air his stumps uplifted high
    So that his visage was with blood besmeared,
And, ' Mosca, too, remember !' loud did cry,
    'Who said, ah me !   " A thing once done is done ! "
    An evil seed for all in Tuscany.'

I added :   ' Yea, and death to every one
    Of thine !' whence he, woe piled on woe, his way   110
    Went like a man with grief demented grown.
But I to watch the gang made longer stay,
    And something saw which I should have a fear,
    Without more proof, so much as even to say,
But that my conscience bids me have good cheer—
    The comrade leal whose friendship fortifies
    A man beneath the mail of purpose clear.
I saw in sooth (still seems it 'fore mine eyes),
    A headless trunk ; with that sad company
    It forward moved, and on the selfsame wise.   120
The severed head, clutched by the hair, swung free
    Down from the fist, yea, lantern-like hung down ;
    Staring at us it murmured :   ' Wretched me !'
A lamp he made of head-piece once his own ;
    And he was two in one and one in two ;
    But how, to Him who thus ordains is known.
Arrived beneath the bridge and full in view,
    With outstretched arm his head he lifted high
    To bring his words well to us.   These I knew :
' Consider well my grievous penalty,   130
    Thou who, though still alive, art visiting
    The people dead ; what pain with this can vie ?
In order that to earth thou news mayst bring
    Of me, that I'm Bertrand de Born know well,
    Who gave bad counsel to the Younger King.
I son and sire made each 'gainst each rebel :
    David and Absalom were fooled not more
    By counsels of the false Ahithophel.
Kinsmen so close since I asunder tore,
    Severed, alas ! I carry now my brain   140
    From what it grew from in this trunk of yore :
And so I prove the law of pain for pain.'

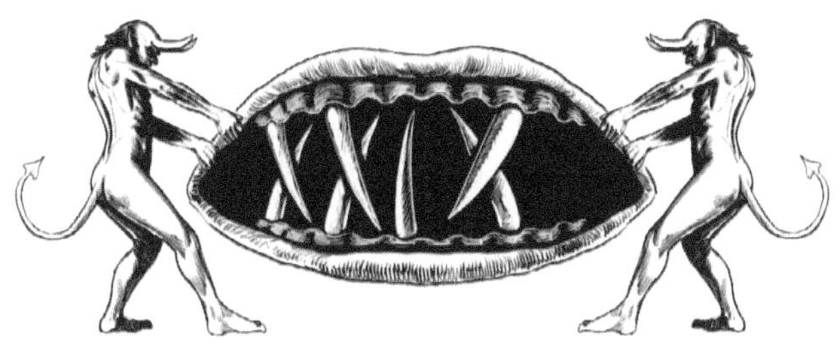

THE MANY FOLK and wounds of divers kind
 Had flushed mine eyes and set them on the flow,
 Till I to weep and linger had a mind ;
But Virgil said to me : ' Why gazing so ?
 Why still thy vision fastening on the crew
 Of dismal shades dismembered there below ?
Thou didst not thus the other Bolgias view :
 Think, if to count them be thine enterprise,
 The valley circles twenty miles and two.
Beneath our feet the moon already lies ;   10
 The time wears fast away to us decreed ;
 And greater things than these await thine eyes.'
I answered swift : ' Hadst thou but given heed
 To why it was my looks were downward bent,
 To yet more stay thou mightest have agreed.'
My Guide meanwhile was moving, and I went
 Behind him and continued to reply,
 Adding : ' Within the moat on which intent
I now was gazing with such eager eye
 I trow a spirit weeps, one of my kin,   20
 The crime whose guilt is rated there so high.'
Then said the Master : ' Henceforth hold thou in
 Thy thoughts from wandering to him : new things claim
 Attention now, so leave him with his sin.
Him saw I at thee from the bridge-foot aim
 A threatening finger, while he made thee known ;
 Geri del Bello heard I named his name.
But, at the time, thou wast with him alone
 Engrossed who once held Hautefort, nor the place
 Didst look at where he was ; so passed he on.'   30

GERI DEL BELLO
Canto XXIX, lines 28 - 42

' O Leader mine ! Death violent and base,
    And not avenged as yet,' I made reply,
    ' By any of his partners in disgrace,
Made him disdainful ; therefore went he by
    And spake not with me, if I judge aright ;
    Which does the more my ruth intensify.'
So we conversed till from the cliff we might
    Of the next valley have had prospect good
    Down to the bottom, with but clearer light.
When we above the inmost Cloister stood   40
    Of Malebolge, and discerned the crew
    Of such as there compose the Brotherhood,
So many lamentations pierced me through—
    And barbed with pity all the shafts were sped—
    My open palms across my ears I drew.
From Valdichiana's every spital bed
    All ailments to September from July,
    With all in Maremma and Sardinia bred,
Heaped in one pit a sickness might supply
    Like what was here ; and from it rose a stink   50
    Like that which comes from limbs that putrefy.
Then we descended by the utmost brink
    Of the long ridge—leftward once more we fell—
    Until my vision, quickened now, could sink
Deeper to where Justice infallible,
    The minister of the Almighty Lord,
    Chastises forgers doomed on earth to Hell.
Ægina could no sadder sight afford,
    As I believe (when all the people ailed
    And all the air was so with sickness stored,   60
Down to the very worms creation failed
    And died, whereon the pristine folk once more,
    As by the poets is for certain held,
From seed of ants their family did restore),
    Than what was offered by that valley black
    With plague-struck spirits heaped upon the floor.
Supine some lay, each on the other's back
    Or stomach ; and some crawled with crouching gait
    For change of place along the doleful track.

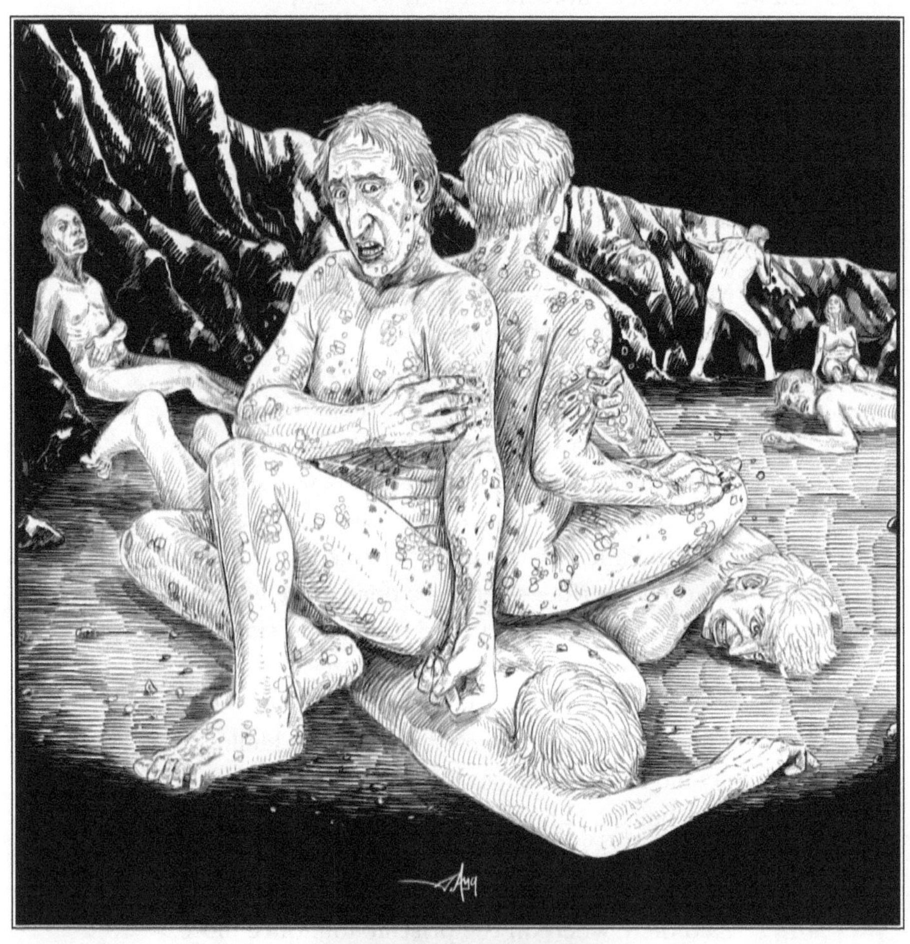

THE FALSIFIERS
Canto XXIX, lines 59 - 88

Speechless we moved with step deliberate,   70
    With eyes and ears on those disease crushed down
    Nor left them power to lift their bodies straight.
I saw two sit, shoulder to shoulder thrown
    As plate holds plate up to be warmed, from head
    Down to the feet with scurf and scab o'ergrown.
Nor ever saw I curry-comb so plied
    By varlet with his master standing by,
    Or by one kept unwillingly from bed,
As I saw each of these his scratchers ply
    Upon himself ; for nought else now avails   80
    Against the itch which plagues them furiously.
The scab they tore and loosened with their nails,
    As with a knife men use the bream to strip,
    Or any other fish with larger scales.
'Thou, that thy mail dost with thy fingers rip.'
    My Guide to one of them began to say,
    'And sometimes dost with them as pincers nip,
Tell, is there any here from Italy
    Among you all, so may thy nails suffice
    For this their work to all eternity.'   90
'Latians are both of us in this disguise
    Of wretchedness,' weeping said one of those ;
    'But who art thou, demanding on this wise ?'
My Guide made answer :   'I am one who goes
    Down with this living man from steep to steep
    That I to him Inferno may disclose.'
Then broke their mutual prop ; trembling with deep
    Amazement each turned to me, with the rest
    To whom his words had echoed in the heap.
Me the good Master cordially addressed :   100
    'Whate'er thou hast a mind to ask them, say.'
    And since he wished it, thus I made request :
'So may remembrance of you not decay
    Within the upper world out of the mind
    Of men, but flourish still for many a day,
As ye shall tell your names and what your kind :
    Let not your vile, disgusting punishment
    To full confession make you disinclined.'

' An Aretine, I to the stake was sent
    By Albert of Siena,' one confessed,   110
    ' But came not here through that for which I went
To death. ' Tis true I told him all in jest,
    I through the air could float in upward gyre ;
    And he, inquisitive and dull at best,
Did full instruction in the art require :
    I could not make him Dædalus, so then
    His second father sent me to the fire.
But to the deepest Bolgia of the ten,
    For alchemy which in the world I wrought,
    The unerring Minos doomed me.' ' Now were men   120
E'er found,' I of the Poet asked, ' so fraught
    With vanity as are the Sienese ?
    French vanity to theirs is surely nought.'
The other leper hearing me, to these
    My words : ' Omit the Stricca,' swift did shout,
    ' Who knew his tastes with temperance to please ;
And Nicholas, who earliest found out
    The lavish custom of the clove-stuffed roast
    Within the garden where such seed doth sprout.
Nor count the club where Caccia d' Ascian lost   130
    Vineyards and woods ; 'mid whom away did throw
    His wit the Abbagliato. But whose ghost
It is, that thou mayst weet, that backs thee so
    Against the Sienese, make sharp thine eyes
    That thou my countenance mayst surely know.
In me Capocchio's shade thou'lt recognise,
    Who forged false coin by means of alchemy :
    Thou must remember, if I well surmise,
How I of nature very ape could be.'

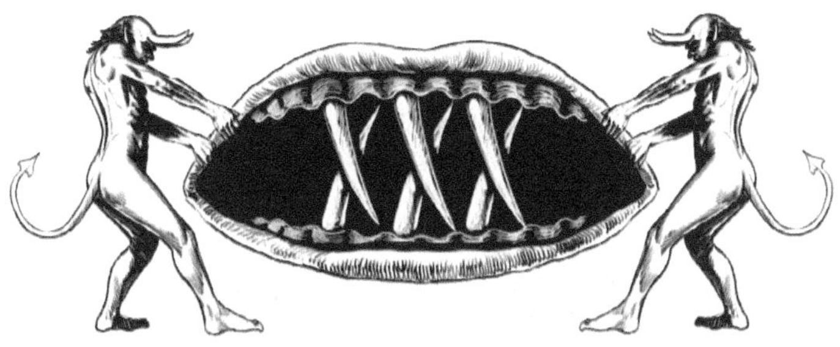

BECAUSE OF SEMELE when Juno's ire
    Was fierce 'gainst all that were to Thebes allied,
    As had been proved by many an instance dire ;
So mad grew Athamas that when he spied
    His wife as she with children twain drew near,
    Each hand by one encumbered, loud he cried :
' Be now the nets outspread, that I may snare
    Cubs with the lioness at yon strait ground !'
    And stretching claws of all compassion bare
He on Learchus seized and swung him round,   10
    And shattered him upon a flinty stone ;
    Then she herself and the other burden drowned.
And when by fortune was all overthrown
    The Trojans' pride, inordinate before—
    Monarch and kingdom equally undone—
Hecuba, sad and captive, mourning o'er
    Polyxena, when dolorous she beheld
    The body of her darling Polydore
Upon the coast, out of her wits she yelled,
    And spent herself in barking like a hound ;   20
    So by her sorrow was her reason quelled.
But never yet was Trojan fury found,
    Nor that of Thebes, to sting so cruelly
    Brute beasts, far less the human form to wound,
As two pale naked shades were stung, whom I
    Saw biting run, like swine when they escape
    Famished and eager from the empty sty.
Capocchio coming up to, in his nape
    One fixed his fangs, and hauling at him made
    His belly on the stony pavement scrape.   30

THE IMPOSTERS
Canto XXX, lines 1 - 39

The Aretine who stood, still trembling, said :
      ' That imp is Gianni Schicchi, and he goes
      Rabid, thus trimming others.'   ' O ! ' I prayed,
' So may the teeth of the other one of those
      Not meet in thee, as, ere she pass from sight,
      Thou freely shalt the name of her disclose.'
And he to me :   ' That is the ancient sprite
      Of shameless Myrrha, who let liking rise
      For him who got her, past all bounds of right.
 As, to transgress with him, she in disguise   40
      Came near to him deception to maintain ;
      So he, departing yonder from our eyes,
That he the Lady of the herd might gain,
      Bequeathed his goods by formal testament
      While he Buoso Donate's form did feign.'
And when the rabid couple from us went,
      Who all this time by me were being eyed,
      Upon the rest ill-starred I grew intent ;
And, fashioned like a lute, I one espied,
      Had he been only severed at the place   50
      Where at the groin men's lower limbs divide.
The grievous dropsy, swol'n with humours base,
      Which every part of true proportion strips
      Till paunch grows out of keeping with the face,
Compelled him widely ope to hold his lips
      Like one in fever who, by thirst possessed,
      Has one drawn up while the other chinward slips.
' O ye ! who by no punishment distressed,
      Nor know I why, are in this world of dool.'
      He said ;   ' a while let your attention rest   60
On Master Adam here of misery full.
      Living, I all I wished enjoyed at will ;
      Now lust I for a drop of water cool.
The water-brooks that down each grassy hill
      Of Casentino to the Arno fall
      And with cool moisture all their courses fill—
Always, and not in vain, I see them all ;
      Because the vision of them dries me more
      Than the disease 'neath which my face grows small.

MASTER ADAM AND SINON
Canto XXX, lines 100 - 129

For rigid justice, me chastising sore,   70
    Can in the place I sinned at motive find
    To swell the sighs in which I now deplore.
There lies Romena, where of the money coined
    With the Baptist's image I made counterfeit,
    And therefore left my body burnt behind.
But could I see here Guido's wretched sprite,
    Or Alexander's, or their brother's, I
    For Fonte Branda would not give the sight.
One is already here, unless they lie—
    Mad souls with power to wander through the crowd—   80
    What boots it me, whose limbs diseases tie ?
But were I yet so nimble that I could
    Creep one poor inch a century, some while
    Ago had I begun to take the road
Searching for him among this people vile ;
    And that although eleven miles 'tis long,
    And has a width of more than half a mile.
Because of them am I in such a throng ;
    For to forge florins I by them was led,
    Which by three carats of alloy were wrong,   90
' Who are the wretches twain,' I to him said,
    ' Who smoke like hand in winter-time fresh brought
    From water, on thy right together spread ?'
' Here found I them, nor have they budged a jot.'
    He said, ' since I was hurled into this vale ;
    And, as I deem, eternally they'll not.
One with false charges Joseph did assail ;
    False Sinon, Greek from Troy, is the other wight.
    Burning with fever they this stink exhale.'
Then one of them, perchance o'ercome with spite   100
    Because he thus contemptuously was named,
    Smote with his fist upon the belly tight.
It sounded like a drum ; and then was aimed
    A blow by Master Adam at his face
    With arm no whit less hard, while he exclaimed :
' What though I can no longer shift my place
    Because my members by disease are weighed !
    I have an arm still free for such a case.'

To which was answered :   ' When thou wast conveyed
    Unto the fire 'twas not thus good at need,   110
    But even more so when the coiner's trade
Was plied by thee.'   The swol'n one :   ' True indeed !
    But thou didst not bear witness half so true
    When Trojan sat thee for the truth did plead.'
' If I spake falsely, thou didst oft renew
    False coin,' said Sinon ;   ' one fault brought me here ;
    Thee more than any devil of the crew.'
' Bethink thee of the horse, thou perjurer.'
    He of the swol'n paunch answered ; ' and that by
    All men 'tis known should anguish in thee stir.'   120
' Be thirst that cracks thy tongue thy penalty,
    And putrid water,' so the Greek replied,
    ' Which 'fore thine eyes thy stomach moundeth high.'
The coiner then :   ' Thy mouth thou openest wide,
    As thou art used, thy slanderous words to vent ;
    But if I thirst and humours plump my hide
Thy head throbs with the fire within thee pent.
    To lap Narcissus' mirror, to implore
    And urge thee on would need no argument.'
While I to hear them did attentive pore   130
    My Master said :   ' Thy fill of staring take !
    To rouse my anger needs but little more.'
And when I heard that he in anger spake
    Toward him I turned with such a shame inspired,
    Recalled, it seems afresh on me to break.
And, as the man who dreams of hurt is fired
    With wish that he might know his dream a dream,
    And so what is, as 'twere not, is desired ;
So I, struck dumb and filled with an extreme
    Craving to find excuse, unwittingly   140
    The meanwhile made the apology supreme.
' Less shame,' my Master said, ' would nullify
    A greater fault, for greater guilt atone ;
    All sadness for it, therefore, lay thou by.
But bear in mind that thou art not alone,
    If fortune hap again to bring thee near
    Where people such debate are carrying on.
To things like these 'tis shame to lend an ear.'

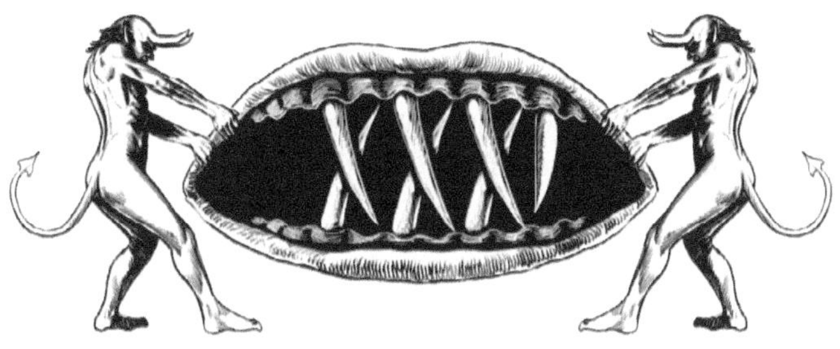

*The Ninth Circle, outside of which they remain till the end of this Canto ✤ the Central Pit of Inferno
encircled and guarded by Giants Nimrod, Ephialtes, and Antæus ✤ entrance to the Pit*

THE VERY TONGUE that first had caused me pain,
    Biting till both my cheeks were crimsoned o'er,
    With healing medicine me restored again.
So have I heard, the lance Achilles bore,
    Which earlier was his father's, first would wound
    And then to health the wounded part restore.
From that sad valley we our backs turned round,
    Up the encircling rampart making way
    Nor uttering, as we crossed it, any sound.
Here was it less than night and less than day,   10
    And scarce I saw at all what lay ahead ;
    But of a trumpet the sonorous bray—
No thunder-peal were heard beside it—led
    Mine eyes along the line by which it passed,
    Till on one spot their gaze concentrated.
When by the dolorous rout was overcast
    The sacred enterprise of Charlemagne
    Roland blew not so terrible a blast.
Short time my head was that way turned, when plain
    I many lofty towers appeared to see.   20
    ' Master, what town is this ?'   I asked.   ' Since fain
Thou art,' he said, ' to pierce the obscurity
    While yet through distance 'tis inscrutable,
    Thou must of error needs the victim be.
Arriving there thou shalt distinguish well
    How much by distance was thy sense betrayed ;
    Therefore to swifter course thyself compel.'
Then tenderly he took my hand, and said :
    ' Ere we pass further I would have thee know,
    That at the fact thou mayst be less dismayed,   30

These are not towers but giants ; in a row
      Set round the brink each in the pit abides,
      His navel hidden and the parts below.'
And even as when the veil of mist divides
      Little by little dawns upon the sight
      What the obscuring vapour earlier hides ;
So, piercing the gross air uncheered by light,
      As I step after step drew near the bound
      My error fled, but I was filled with fright.
As Montereggion with towers is crowned   40
      Which from the walls encircling it arise ;
      So, rising from the pit's encircling mound,
Half of their bodies towered before mine eyes—
      Dread giants, still by Jupiter defied
      From Heaven whene'er it thunders in the skies.
The face of one already I descried,
      His shoulders, breast, and down his belly far,
      And both his arms dependent by his side.
When Nature ceased such creatures as these are
      To form, she of a surety wisely wrought   50
      Wresting from Mars such ministers of war.
And though she rue not that to life she brought
      The whale and elephant, who deep shall read
      Will justify her wisdom in his thought ;
For when the powers of intellect are wed
      To strength and evil will, with them made one,
      The race of man is helpless left indeed.
As large and long as is St. Peter's cone
      At Rome, the face appeared ; of every limb
      On scale like this was fashioned every bone.   60
So that the bank, which covered half of him
      As might a tunic, left uncovered yet
      So much that if to his hair they sought to climb
Three Frisians end on end their match had met ;
      For thirty great palms I of him could see,
      Counting from where a man's cloak-clasp is set.
Rafelmai amech zabi almi !
      Out of the bestial mouth began to roll,
      Which scarce would suit more dulcet psalmody.

NIMROD, EPHIALTES, AND ANTÆUS
Canto XXI, lines 41 - 136

And then my Leader charged him :   ' Stupid soul,   70
     Stick to thy horn.   With it relieve thy mind
     When rage or other passions pass control.
Feel at thy neck, round which the thong is twined
     O puzzle-headed wretch ! from which 'tis slung ;
     Clipping thy monstrous breast thou shalt it find.'
And then to me :   ' From his own mouth is wrung
     Proof of his guilt.   ' Tis Nimrod, whose insane
     Whim hindered men from speaking in one tongue.
Leave we him here nor spend our speech in vain ;
     For words to him in any language said,   80
     As unto others his, no sense contain.'
Turned to the left, we on our journey sped,
     And at the distance of an arrow's flight
     We found another huger and more dread.
By what artificer thus pinioned tight
     I cannot tell, but his left arm was bound
     In front, as at his back was bound the right,
By a chain which girt him firmly round and round ;
     About what of his frame there was displayed
     Below the neck, in fivefold gyre 'twas wound.   90
' Incited by ambition this one made
     Trial of prowess 'gainst Almighty Jove.'
     My Leader told, ' and he is thus repaid.
'Tis Ephialtes, mightily who strove
     What time the giants to the gods caused fright :
     The arms he wielded then no more will move.'
And I to him :   ' Fain would I, if I might,
     On the enormous Briareus set eye,
     And know the truth by holding him in sight.'
' Antæus thou shalt see,' he made reply,   100
     ' Ere long, and he can speak, nor is in chains.
     Us to the depth of all iniquity
He shall let down.   The one thou'dst see remains
     Far off, like this one bound and like in make,
     But in his face far more of fierceness reigns.'
Never when earth most terribly did quake
     Shook any tower so much as what all o'er
     And suddenly did Ephialtes shake.

Terror of death possessed me more and more ;
  The fear alone had served my turn indeed,
  But that I marked the ligatures he wore.
Then did we somewhat further on proceed,
  Reaching Antæus who for good five ell,
  His head not counted, from the pit was freed.
' O thou who from the fortune-haunted dell—
  Where Scipio of glory was made heir
  When with his host to flight turned Hannibal—
A thousand lions didst for booty bear
  Away, and who, hadst thou but joined the host
  And like thy brethren fought, some even aver
The victory to earth's sons had not been lost,
  Lower us now, nor disobliging show,
  To where Cocytus fettered is by frost.
To Tityus nor to Typhon make us go.
  To grant what here is longed for he hath power,
  Cease them to curl thy snout, but bend thee low.
He can for wage thy name on earth restore ;
  He lives, and still expecteth to live long,
  If Grace recall him not before his hour.'
So spake my Master.   Then his hands he swung
  Downward and seized my Leader in all haste—
  Hands in whose grip even Hercules once was wrung.
And Virgil when he felt them round him cast
  Said :   ' That I may embrace thee, hither tend.'
  And in one bundle with him made me fast.
And as to him that under Carisend
  Stands on the side it leans to, while clouds fly
  Counter its slope, the tower appears to bend ;
Even so to me who stood attentive by
  Antæus seemed to stoop, and I, dismayed,
  Had gladly sought another road to try.
But us in the abyss he gently laid,
  Where Lucifer and Judas gulfed remain ;
  Nor to it thus bent downward long time stayed,
But like a ship's mast raised himself again.

110

120

130

140

LIFTED OVER THE WALL
Canto XXXI, lines 139 - 145

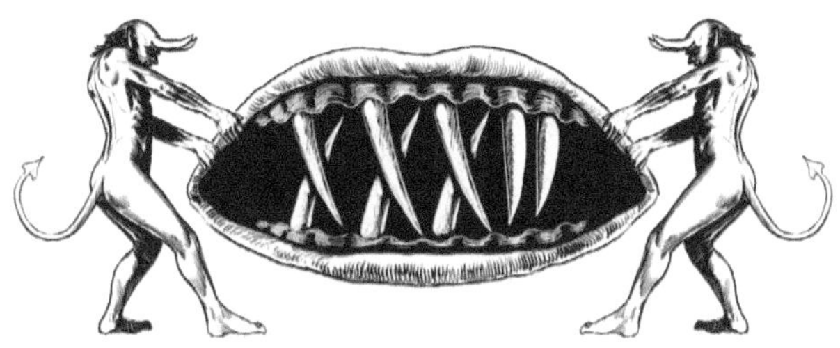

The Ninth Circle ✠ that of the Traitors, is divided into four concentric rings, in which the sinners are plunged more or less deep in the ice of the frozen Cocytus ✠ the Outer Ring is Caïna, where are those who contrived the murder of their Kindred ✠ Camicion de' Pazzi ✠ Antenora, the Second Ring, where are such as betrayed their Country ✠ Bocca degli Abati ✠ Buoso da Duera ✠ Ugolino

HAD I SONOROUS ROUGH RHYMES at command,
    Such as would suit the cavern terrible
    Rooted on which all the other ramparts stand,
The sap of fancies which within me swell
    Closer I'd press ; but since I have not these,
    With some misgiving I go on to tell.
For 'tis no task to play with as you please,
    Of all the world the bottom to portray,
    Nor one that with a baby speech agrees.
But let those ladies help me with my lay   10
    Who helped Amphion walls round Thebes to pile,
    And faithful to the facts my words shall stay.
O 'bove all creatures wretched, for whose vile
    Abode 'tis hard to find a language fit,
    As sheep or goats ye had been happier !   While
We still were standing in the murky pit—
    Beneath the giant's feet set far below—
    And at the high wall I was staring yet,
When this I heard :   ' Heed to thy steps bestow,
    Lest haply by thy soles the heads be spurned   20
    Of wretched brothers wearied in their woe.'
Before me, as on hearing this I turned,
    Beneath my feet a frozen lake, its guise
    Rather of glass than water, I discerned.
In all its course on Austrian Danube lies
    No veil in time of winter near so thick,
    Nor on the Don beneath its frigid skies,
As this was here ; on which if Tabernicch
    Or Mount Pietrapana should alight
    Not even the edge would answer with a creak.   30

And as the croaking frog holds well in sight
    Its muzzle from the pool, what time of year
    The peasant girl of gleaning dreams at night ;
The mourning shades in ice were covered here,
    Seen livid up to where we blush with shame.
    In stork-like music their teeth chattering were.
With downcast face stood every one of them :
    To cold from every mouth, and to despair
    From every eye, an ample witness came.
And having somewhat gazed around me there   40
    I to my feet looked down, and saw two pressed
    So close together, tangled was their hair,
' Say, who are you with breast thus strained to breast ?'
    I asked ; whereon their necks they backward bent,
    And when their upturned faces lay at rest
Their eyes, which earlier were but moistened, sent
    Tears o'er their eyelids : these the frost congealed
    And fettered fast before they further went.
Plank set to plank no rivet ever held
    More firmly ; wherefore, goat-like, either ghost   50
    Butted the other ; so their wrath prevailed.
And one who wanted both ears, which the frost
    Had bitten off, with face still downward thrown,
    Asked : ' Why with us art thou so long engrossed ?
If who that couple are thou'dst have made known—
    The vale down which Bisenzio's floods decline
    Was once their father Albert's and their own.
One body bore them : search the whole malign
    Caïna, and thou shalt not any see
    More worthy to be fixed in gelatine ;   60
Not he whose breast and shadow equally
    Were by one thrust of Arthur's lance pierced through :
    Nor yet Focaccia ; nor the one that me
With his head hampers, blocking out my view,
    Whose name was Sassol Mascheroni : well
    Thou must him know if thou art Tuscan too.
And that thou need'st not make me further tell—
    I'm Camicion de' Pazzi,and Carlin
    I weary for, whose guilt shall mine excel.'

A thousand faces saw I dog-like grin,70
Frost-bound ; whence I, as now, shall always shake
Whenever sight of frozen pools I win.
While to the centre we our way did make
To which all things converging gravitate,
And me that chill eternal caused to quake ;
Whether by fortune, providence, or fate,
I know not, but as 'mong the heads I went
I kicked one full in the face ; who therefore straight
' Why trample on me ?' Snarled and made lament,
' Unless thou com'st to heap the vengeance high80
For Montaperti, why so virulent
'Gainst me ?' I said : ' Await me here till I
By him, O Master, shall be cleared of doubt ;
Then let my pace thy will be guided by.'
My Guide delayed, and I to him spake out,
While he continued uttering curses shrill :
' Say, what art thou, at others thus to shout ?'
' But who art thou, that goest at thy will
Through Antenora, trampling on the face
Of others ? 'Twere too much if thou wert still90
In life.' ' I live, and it may help thy case.'
Was my reply, ' if thou renown wouldst gain,
Should I thy name upon my tablets place.'
And he : ' I for the opposite am fain.
Depart thou hence, nor work me further dool ;
Within this swamp thou flatterest all in vain.'
Then I began him by the scalp to pull,
And ' Thou must tell how thou art called,' I said,
' Or soon thy hair will not be plentiful.'
And he : ' Though every hair thou from me shred100
I will not tell thee, nor my face turn round ;
No, though a thousand times thou spurn my head.'
His locks ere this about my fist were wound,
And many a tuft I tore, while dog-like wails
Burst from him, and his eyes still sought the ground.
Then called another : ' Bocca, what now ails ?
Is't not enough thy teeth go chattering there,
But thou must bark ? What devil thee assails ?'

ANTENORA
Canto XXXII, lines 74 - 93

' Ah ! Now,' said I, ' thou need'st not aught declare,
    Accursed traitor ; and true news of thee 110
    To thy disgrace I to the world will bear.'
' Begone, tell what thou wilt,' he answered me ;
    ' But, if thou issue hence, not silent keep
    Of him whose tongue but lately wagged so free.
He for the Frenchmen's money here doth weep.
    Him of Duera saw I, mayst thou tell,
    Where sinners shiver in the frozen deep.
Shouldst thou be asked who else within it dwell—
    Thou hast the Beccheria at thy side ;
    Across whose neck the knife at Florence fell. 120
John Soldanieri may be yonder spied
    With Ganellon, and Tribaldell who threw
    Faenza's gates, when slept the city, wide.'
Him had we left, our journey to pursue,
    When frozen in a hole a pair I saw ;
    One's head like the other's hat showed to the view.
And, as their bread men hunger-driven gnaw,
    The uppermost tore fiercely at his mate
    Where nape and brain-pan to a junction draw.
No worse by Tydeus in his scornful hate 130
    Were Menalippus' temples gnawed and hacked
    Than skull and all were torn by him irate.
' O thou who provest by such bestial act
    Hatred of him who by thy teeth is chewed,
    Declare thy motive,' said I, ' on this pact—
That if with reason thou with him hast feud,
    Knowing your names and manner of his crime
    I in the world to thee will make it good ;
If what I speak with dry not ere the time.'

SINNER'S SAVAGE FEAST
Canto XXXIII, lines 1 - 15

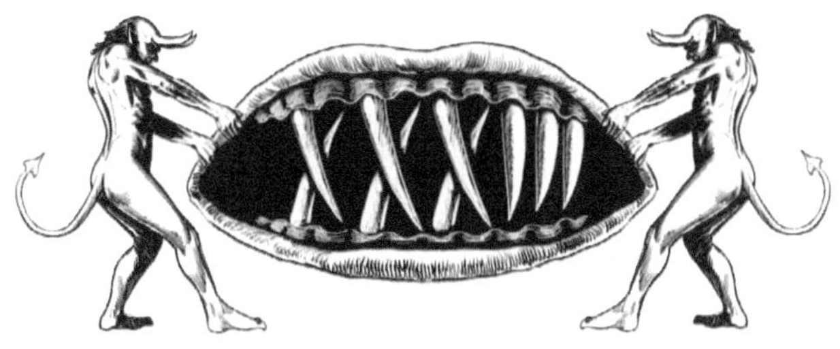

HIS MOUTH UPLIFTING from the savage feast,
    The sinner rubbed and wiped it free of gore
    On the hair of the head he from behind laid waste ;
And then began : ' Thou'dst have me wake once more
    A desperate grief, of which to think alone,
    Ere I have spoken, wrings me to the core.
But if my words shall be as seed that sown
    May fructify unto the traitor's shame
    Whom thus I gnaw, I mingle speech and groan.
Of how thou earnest hither or thy name   10
    I nothing know, but that a Florentine
    In very sooth thou art, thy words proclaim.
Thou then must know I was Count Ugolin,
    The Archbishop Roger he.   Now hearken well
    Why I prove such a neighbour.   How in fine,
And flowing from his ill designs, it fell
    That I, confiding in his words, was caught
    Then done to death, were waste of time to tell.
But that of which as yet thou heardest nought
    Is how the death was cruel which I met :   20
    Hearken and judge if wrong to me he wrought.
Scant window in the mew whose epithet
    Of Famine came from me its resident,
    And cooped in which shall many languish yet,
Had shown me through its slit how there were spent
    Full many moons, ere that bad dream I dreamed
    When of my future was the curtain rent.
Lord of the hunt and master this one seemed,
    Chasing the wolf and wolf-cubs on the height
    By which from Pisan eyes is Lucca hemmed.   30

With famished hounds well trained and swift of flight,
    Lanfranchi and Gualandi in the van,
    And Sismond he had set.   Within my sight
Both sire and sons—nor long the chase—began
    To grow (so seemed it) weary as they fled ;
    Then through their flanks fangs sharp and eager ran.
When I awoke before the morning spread
    I heard my sons all weeping in their sleep—
    For they were with me—and they asked for bread.
Ah ! cruel if thou canst from pity keep   40
    At the bare thought of what my heart foreknew ;
    And if thou weep'st not, what could make thee weep ?
Now were they 'wake, and near the moment drew
    At which 'twas used to bring us our repast ;
    But each was fearful lest his dream came true.
And then I heard the under gate made fast
    Of the horrible tower, and thereupon I gazed
    In my sons' faces, silent and aghast.
I did not weep, for I to stone was dazed :
    They wept, and darling Anselm me besought :   50
    " What ails thee, father ?   Wherefore thus amazed ?"
And yet I did not weep, and answered not
    The whole day, and that night made answer none,
    Till on the world another sun shone out.
Soon as a feeble ray of light had won
    Into our doleful prison, made aware
    Of the four faces featured like my own,
Both of my hands I bit at in despair ;
    And they, imagining that I was fain
    To eat, arose before me with the prayer :   60
" O father, 'twere for us an easier pain
    If thou wouldst eat us.   Thou didst us array
    In this poor flesh : unclothe us now again."
I calmed me, not to swell their woe.   That day
    And the next day no single word we said.
    Ah ! Pitiless earth, that didst unyawning stay !
When we had reached the fourth day, Gaddo, spread
    Out at my feet, fell prone ; and made demand :
    " Why, O my father, offering us no aid ?"

There died he.   Plain as I before thee stand 70
    I saw the three as one by one they failed,
    The fifth day and the sixth ; then with my hand,
Blind now, I groped for each of them, and wailed
    On them for two days after they were gone.
    Famine at last, more strong than grief, prevailed.'
When he had uttered this, his eyes all thrown
    Awry, upon the hapless skull he fell
    With teeth that, dog-like, rasped upon the bone.
Ah, Pisa ! byword of the folk that dwell
    In the sweet country where the *Si* doth sound, 80
    Since slow thy neighbours to reward thee well
Let now Gorgona and Capraia mound
    Themselves where Arno with the sea is blent,
    Till every one within thy walls be drowned.
For though report of Ugolino went
    That he betrayed thy castles, thou didst wrong
    Thus cruelly his children to torment.
These were not guilty, for they were but young,
    Thou modern Thebes ! Brigata and young Hugh,
    And the other twain of whom above 'tis sung. 90
We onward passed to where another crew
    Of shades the thick-ribbed ice doth fettered keep ;
    Their heads not downward these, but backward threw.
Their very weeping will not let them weep,
    And grief, encountering barriers at their eyes,
    Swells, flowing inward, their affliction deep ;
For the first tears that issue crystallise,
    And fill, like vizor fashioned out of glass,
    The hollow cup o'er which the eyebrows rise.
And though, as 'twere a callus, now my face 100
    By reason of the frost was wholly grown
    Benumbed and dead to feeling, I could trace
(So it appeared), a breeze against it blown,
    And asked :   ' O Master, whence comes this ?   So low
    As where we are is any vapour known ?'
And he replied :   ' Thou ere long while shalt go
    Where touching this thine eye shall answer true,
    Discovering that which makes the wind to blow.'

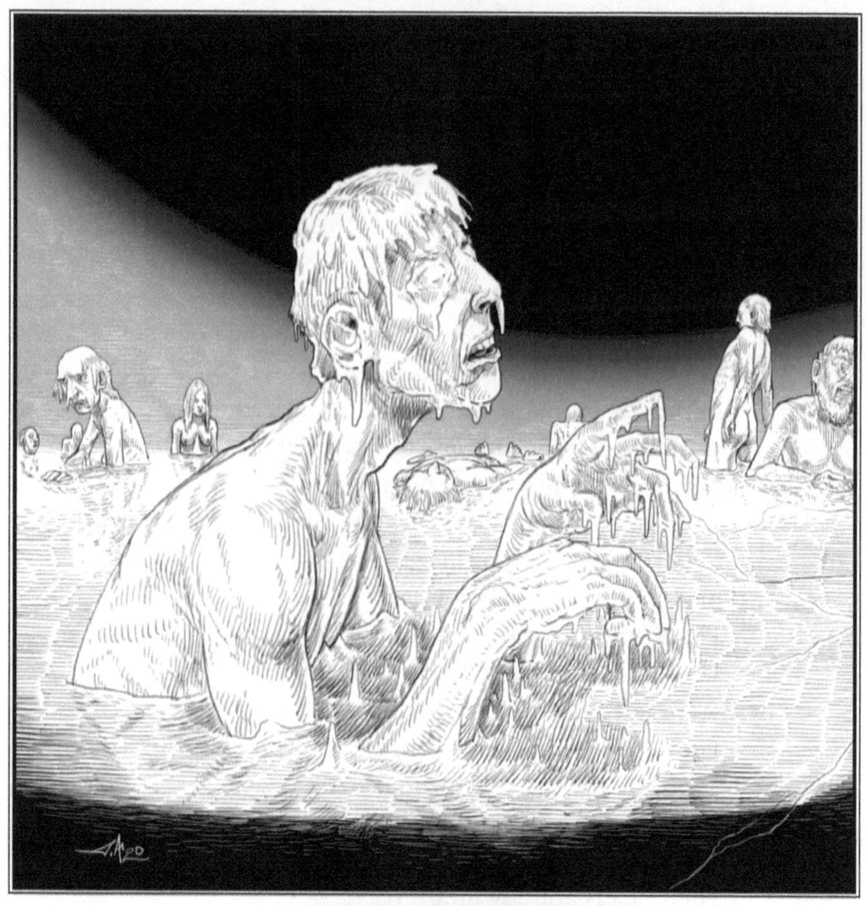

PTOLOMÆA
Canto XXXIII, lines 74 - 93

Then from the cold crust one of that sad crew
    Demanded loud : 'Spirits, for whom they hold   110
    The inmost room, so truculent were you,
Back from my face let these hard veils be rolled
    That I may vent the woe which chokes my heart,
    Ere tears again solidify with cold.'
And I to him : 'First tell me who thou art
    If thou'dst have help ; then if I help not quick
    To the bottom of the ice let me depart.'
He answered : 'I am Friar Alberic—
    He of the fruit grown in the orchard fell—
    And here am I repaid with date for fig.'   120

‘ Ah !’ said I to him, ‘ art thou dead as well ?’
    ‘ How now my body fares,’ he answered me,
    ‘ Up in the world, I have no skill to tell ;
For Ptolomæa has this quality—
    The soul oft plunges hither to its place
    Ere it has been by Atropos set free.
And that more willingly from off my face
    Thou mayst remove the glassy tears, know, soon
    As ever any soul of man betrays
As I betrayed, the body once his own   130
    A demon takes and governs until all
    The span allotted for his life be run.
Into this tank headlong the soul doth fall ;
    And on the earth his body yet may show
    Whose shade behind me wintry frosts enthral.
But thou canst tell, if newly come below :
    It is Ser Branca d’Oria, and complete
    Is many a year since he was fettered so.’
‘ It seems,’ I answered, ‘ that thou wouldst me cheat,
    For Branca d’Oria never can have died :   140
    He sleeps, puts clothes on, swallows drink and meat.’
‘ Or e’er to the tenacious pitchy tide
    Which boils in Malebranche’s moat had come
    The shade of Michael Zanche,’ he replied,
‘ That soul had left a devil in its room
    Within its body ; of his kinsmen one
    Treacherous with him experienced equal doom.
But stretch thy hand and be its work begun
    Of setting free mine eyes.’   This did not I.
    Twas highest courtesy to yield him none.   150
Ah, Genoese, strange to morality !
    Ye men infected with all sorts of sin !
    Out of the world ’tis time that ye should die.
Here, to Romagna’s blackest soul akin,
    I chanced on one of you ; for doing ill
    His soul o’erwhelmed Cocytus’ floods within,
Though in the flesh he seems surviving still.

LUCIFER
Canto XXXIV, lines 14 - 33

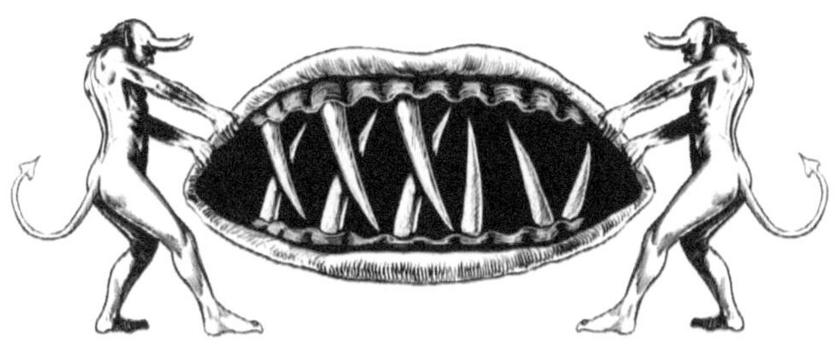

The Ninth Circle ⁃ the Fourth Ring or Judecca, the deepest point of the Inferno and the Centre of the Universe ⁃ it is the place of those treacherous to their Lords or Benefactors ⁃ Lucifer with Judas, Brutus, and Cassius hanging from his mouths ⁃ passage through the Centre of the Earth ⁃ ascent from the depths to the light of the stars in the Southern Hemisphere

'*Vexilla Regis prodeunt Inferni*
  Towards where we are ; seek then with vision keen.'
  My Master bade, ' if trace of him thou spy.'
As, when the exhalations dense have been,
  Or when our hemisphere grows dark with night,
  A windmill from afar is sometimes seen,
I seemed to catch of such a structure sight ;
  And then to 'scape the blast did backward draw
  Behind my Guide—sole shelter in my plight.
Now was I where (I versify with awe)   10
  The shades were wholly covered, and did show
  Visible as in glass are bits of straw.
Some stood upright and some were lying low,
  Some with head topmost, others with their feet ;
  And some with face to feet bent like a bow.
But we kept going on till it seemed meet
  Unto my Master that I should behold
  The creature once of countenance so sweet.
He stepped aside and stopped me as he told :
  ' Lo, Dis !   And lo, we are arrived at last   20
  Where thou must nerve thee and must make thee bold.'
How I hereon stood shivering and aghast,
  Demand not, Reader ; this I cannot write ;
  So much the fact all reach of words surpassed.
I was not dead, yet living was not quite :
  Think for thyself, if gifted with the power,
  What, life and death denied me, was my plight.
Of that tormented realm the Emperor
  Out of the ice stood free to middle breast ;
  And me a giant less would overtower   30

Than would his arm a giant.   By such test
    Judge then what bulk the whole of him must show,
    Of true proportion with such limb possessed.
If he was fair of old as hideous now,
    And yet his brows against his Maker raised,
    Meetly from him doth all affliction flow.
O how it made me horribly amazed
    When on his head I saw three faces grew !
    The one vermilion which straight forward gazed ;
And joining on to it were other two,   40
    One rising up from either shoulder-bone,
    Till to a junction on the crest they drew.
'Twixt white and yellow seemed the right-hand one ;
    The left resembled them whose country lies
    Where valleywards the floods of Nile flow down.
Beneath each face two mighty wings did rise,
    Such as this bird tremendous might demand :
    Sails of sea-ships ne'er saw I of such size.
Not feathered were they, but in style were planned
    Like a bat's wing : by them a threefold breeze—   50
    For still he flapped them—evermore was fanned,
And through its depths Cocytus caused to freeze.
    Down three chins tears for ever made descent
    From his six eyes ; and red foam mixed with these.
In every mouth there was a sinner rent
    By teeth that shred him as a heckle would ;
    Thus three at once compelled he to lament.
To the one in front 'twas little to be chewed
    Compared with being clawed and clawed again,
    Till his back-bone of skin was sometimes nude.   60
' The soul up yonder in the greater pain
    Is Judas 'Scariot, with his head among
    The teeth,' my Master said, ' while outward strain
His legs.   Of the two whose heads are downward hung,
    Brutus is from the black jowl pendulous :
    See how he writhes, yet never wags his tongue.
The other, great of thew, is Cassius :
    But night is rising and we must be gone ;
    For everything hath now been seen by us.'

Then, as he bade, I to his neck held on 70
    While he the time and place of vantage chose ;
    And when the wings enough were open thrown
He grasped the shaggy ribs and clutched them close,
    And so from tuft to tuft he downward went
    Between the tangled hair and crust which froze.
We to the bulging haunch had made descent,
    To where the hip-joint lies in it ; and then
    My Guide, with painful twist and violent,
Turned round his head to where his feet had been,
    And like a climber closely clutched the hair : 80
    I thought to Hell that we returned again.
' Hold fast to me ; it needs by such a stair.'
    Panting, my Leader said, like man foredone,
    ' That we from all that wretchedness repair.'
Right through a hole in a rock when he had won,
    The edge of it he gave me for a seat
    And deftly then to join me clambered on.
I raised mine eyes, expecting they would meet
    With Lucifer as I beheld him last,
    But saw instead his upturned legs and feet. 90
If in perplexity I then was cast,
    Let ignorant people think who do not see
    What point it was that I had lately passed.
' Rise to thy feet,' my Master said to me ;
    ' The way is long and rugged the ascent,
    And at mid tierce the sun must almost be.'
'twas not as if on palace floors we went :
    A dungeon fresh from nature's hand was this ;
    Rough underfoot, and of light indigent.
' Or ever I escape from the abyss, 100
    O Master,' said I, standing now upright,
    ' Correct in few words where I think amiss.
Where lies the ice ?   How hold we him in sight
    Set upside down ?   The sun, how had it skill
    In so short while to pass to morn from night ?'
And he :   ' In fancy thou art standing, still,
    On yon side of the centre, where I caught
    The vile worm's hair which through the world doth drill.

LUCIFER DEVOURING JUDAS, BRUTUS, AND CASSIUS

Canto XXXIV, lines 127 - 139

There wast thou while our downward course I wrought ;
    But when I turned, the centre was passed by   110
    Which by all weights from every point is sought.
And now thou standest 'neath the other sky,
    Opposed to that which vaults the great dry ground
    And 'neath whose summit there did whilom die
The Man whose birth and life were sinless found.
    Thy feet are firm upon the little sphere,
    On this side answering to Judecca's round.
'Tis evening yonder when 'tis morning here ;
    And he whose tufts our ladder rungs supplied.
    Fixed as he was continues to appear.   120
Headlong from Heaven he fell upon this side ;
    Whereon the land, protuberant here before,
    For fear of him did in the ocean hide,
And 'neath our sky emerged : land, as of yore
    Still on this side, perhaps that it might shun
    His fall, heaved up, and filled this depth no more.'
From Belzebub still widening up and on,
    Far-stretching as the sepulchre, extends
    A region not beheld, but only known
By murmur of a brook which through it wends,   130
    Declining by a channel eaten through
    The flinty rock ; and gently it descends.
My Guide and I, our journey to pursue
    To the bright world, upon this road concealed
    Made entrance, and no thought of resting knew.
He first, I second, still ascending held
    Our way until the fair celestial train
    Was through an opening round to me revealed :
And, issuing thence, we saw the stars again.

SIGHT OF THE STARS
Canto XXXIV, lines 127 - 139

AFTERWORD

*J*IM *A*GPALZA

You might be asking yourself why did Jim do Dante's Inferno? Since I was a kid, I've always been fascinated by religious art, especially art that dealt with gods, demons, and the devil—drawn to other cultures and religions with different deities. There are so many ways to depict them. It's always fun to sketch them and put my stink on them.

After reading my copy of Dante's Inferno, I looked up art made for it. I inevitably came across Gustav Dore's epic etchings, and man, how do you do it better than him? Heavily influenced by Dore, the difference between us is I didn't have the church looking over my shoulder. I have no constraints. I have no regrets.

I hope you've enjoyed my renditions of hell. Maybe we'll see each other there soon.

*J*AMES *R*OMANES *S*IBBALD

translator

No known biography is available.

Rev. Henry Francis Cary, M. A.

translator/canto arguements

Henry Francis Cary was an English author and translator who is best known for his blank verse translation of The Divine Comedy, which he completed in 1812.

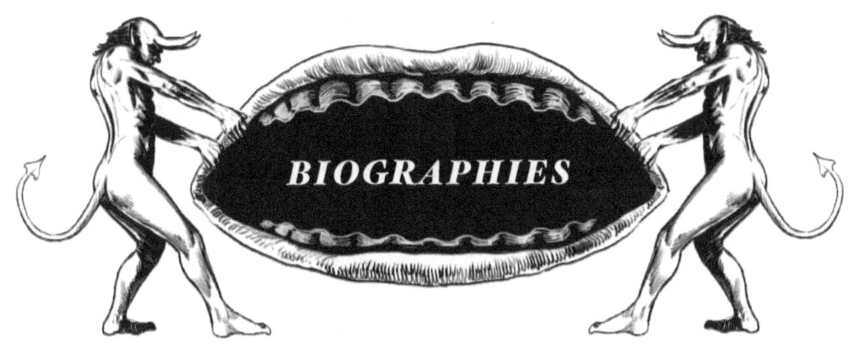

DANTE ALIGHIERI

poet

Dante Alighieri was a poet, writer, and philosopher from Florence, Italy. His Divine Comedy is one of the essential poems in the Middle Ages and is widely considered one of the most significant literary works in all Italian literature.

JIM AGPALZA

illustrator

Jim Agpalza is an artist who resides in Portland, Oregon, with his wife, two kids, and two cats (one is a ghost). He spends most of his time making art, and in his spare time, he takes long walks on the beach and ends each walk with a cuddle with a boulder on the sand.

www.ingramcontent.com/pod-product-compliance
Lightning Source LLC
Chambersburg PA
CBHW021316190726
48288CB00003B/867